CONTENTS

YOUR MUMMY IS A NOSE PICKER

Gordon Korman

Illustrated by **Victor Vaccaro**

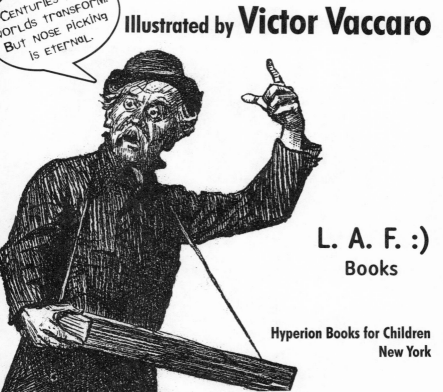

CENTURIES PASS. WORLDS TRANSFORM. BUT NOSE PICKING IS ETERNAL.

L. A. F. :)
Books

Hyperion Books for Children
New York

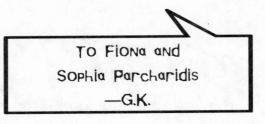

TO FiONa aNd
SoPHia ParcHaridis
—G.K.

For SaraH—V.V.

For information address Hyperion Paperbacks for Children,
114 Fifth Avenue, New York, New York 10011-5690.

First Edition
1 3 5 7 9 10 8 6 4 2

Library of Congress Cataloging-in-Publication Data
Korman, Gordon
Your mummy is a nose picker/by Gordon Korman;
illustrated by Victor Vaccaro.—1st ed.
p. cm.—(L.A.F. Books)
Summary: Devin and his alien visitor Stan from the planet Pan
travel back to ancient Egypt in search of the Nile Delta goldenrod
which will save Stan's job by ensuring that all Pant tourists
on Earth sneeze.
ISBN 0-7868-1446-2 (pbk. ed.)—ISBN 0-7868-2587-1 (lib. ed.)
[1. Extraterrestrial beings—Fiction. 2. Time travel—Fiction. 3.
Egypt—Fiction.] I. Vaccaro, Victor, ill. II. Title. III. Series.
PZ7.K8369Yo 2000
[Fic]—dc21
00-29597

Chapter 1
THE SCHNOZ·AHOLIC

✳ DEVIN HUNTER'S RULES OF COOLNESS ✳

☛ **Rule 25:** Don't give up, even when time is running out on you.

There could never be a better example of that than right now. The National Student Exchange Program was over. For the past three weeks, most of the fourth graders in our school had been hosting kids from other states. Now, as the visitors lined up to get on the bus to the airport, there were some emotional good-byes. Calista Bernstein hugged her partner, Wanda, and promised to E-mail her in California every day. Sam, a soccer nut from Minnesota, was heading a ball back and forth with his host, Tanner Phelps. Cody from Texas presented Joey Petrillo with a really cool brass belt buckle in the shape of the Lone Star State. And my exchange buddy, Stan Mflxnys, had his finger up his nose.

"Oh, *yuck!*" exclaimed Calista. "Stan, cut it out!"

Tanner groaned. "You're wasting your breath, Calista. The kid's a schnoz-aholic. Lucky for us, he'll be back in Pan tonight, where nose picking is the official town sport."

Tanner was our class bigmouth. But he was wrong on four counts. First, Stan wasn't a kid; he was a 147-year-old alien. Second, Pan wasn't a town in Illinois; it was a planet in outer space.

People from Pan are called Pants. Their president is the Grand Pant. His assistants are the Under-Pants. Their planet orbits a star in the constellation of the Big Zipper. It may sound like a comedy routine, but it's one hundred percent true. Stan even took me there once. I saw it with my own eyes.

Third, Stan wasn't really picking his nose. He was operating the tiny supercomputer that Pants

OF COURSE!

have up their nasal cavities. A single nasal processor is stronger than all the

2

millions of computers on Earth put together. It does a lot more than word processing and surfing the Internet. With it, you can cut your lawn without ever touching a mower, or do your homework like magic. A nasal processor can cook a three-minute egg in a trillionth of a second. It's also a built-in cell phone—one that can call anywhere in the galaxy. Even home to Pan, eighty-five thousand light-years away.

Last but not least, Stan wasn't leaving. His assignment here on Earth had just begun. Stan was a travel agent, which is a very important job on Pan. Pants are the greatest tourists in the universe. They work two weeks per year and go on vacation for the other fifty—all except the employees of the Pan-Pan Travel Bureau. They spend all their time searching for new places for Pants to visit.

Stan was a great travel agent, too. Thanks to him, Earth was now Pan's newest resort planet, even though no one on Earth knew about it except me. Pants go on vacation in secret. Even now, there are Pant tourists on thousands of planets, pretending to be locals and taking in the sights.

Shhh! I'M gOiNg ON vaCaTiON. . . .

These days, Earth was the hot spot. Every comet, nebula, and quasar in the galaxy had a billboard encouraging Pants to spend their hard-earned pantaloons on a trip here. Each day, spaceship-loads of tourists were landing on every continent, ready to explore, relax, and party. And Stan was in charge of it all.

But now that the exchange program was over,

Stan had no reason to hang around Clearview anymore. He was supposed to leave, but he needed to stay. My house was his base of operations. I was the only Earthling who knew what Stan really was, so I was the only one who could work with him. A copy of my Rules of Coolness was being sent by nasal processor to every single Pant tourist. That was really important, because even though Pants are far more advanced than

we humans are, they really aren't very cool at all. They need help passing as Earthlings. I mean, even though Stan was my best friend, I had to admit that I'd never met a bigger nerd in my whole life.

It wasn't just the nose picking. Fashion was a little backward on Pan, too. Crew cuts were all the rage, along with glasses so thick that they make your eyes look like fried eggs. Pants' favorite food is paper. Their most popular leisure-time activity is sneezing—it has something to do with having a supercomputer up your nose. The hottest style in clothes is white dress shirts and polka-dot ties. A few of the Pants who have been living on Earth for years have learned to fit in a little better. But after a whole month here, **Stan still looked as if his picture belonged in the dictionary next to the word *dweeb*.**

So that was the problem. How could we keep Stan in Clearview to continue his work as the head travel agent on Earth?

Chapter 2
A MODEL PARENT

The last-minute handshakes were in full swing as we said good-bye to the visitors. Except Stan, that is. When you spend so much time with your finger up your nose, nobody wants to shake your hand.

> HErE, shakE MY gLOVEd haNd!

Uh-oh! The other exchange buddies were filing onto the bus. I shuffled Stan to the back of the line. But what would we do once everybody else was on board?

Our teacher, Mr. Slomin, blew his whistle. "It's been a wonderful month," he announced. "I hope you'll go back to your home states and tell everybody about the warm welcome you received in good old Clearview, a very classy town—Stan, stop picking your nose!"

Stan dropped his hand. "Sorry, Mr. Slomin."

7

But of course Stan wasn't really picking. He was surfing the Pant Internet, the Overall. We had to find a Pant on Earth who was willing to come and pretend to be Stan's parent. Then he or she could ask Mr. Slomin if Stan could please remain in Clearview longer.

"Any luck?" I whispered.

"I, Stan, put out an APB."

I was impressed. "You mean an All Points Bulletin—like the police?"

He shook his head. "This is an All *Pants* Bulletin—wait!" He turned away from our teacher and stuck his finger up his nose again. "Good news. Agent Crfrdnys has responded to my APB. She's on her way now."

"I hope you told her to *hurry*," I hissed. "There's only one person in line ahead of you!"

Then it was Stan's turn. I broke about ten of my rules of coolness trying to stall for time. "Oh, Stan!" I wailed. "Don't go!"

I tried everything. I cried. I hugged him. I even threw myself to the ground and clamped my arms around his ankles. Then and there, I thought of a new rule to add when I got back to

my notebook: ☞ **Rule 102:** Don't make a fool of yourself in front of your entire class.

"All right, Devin," ordered Mr. Slomin. "That's enough. People have flights to catch." He disentangled me from Stan and led him onto the bus.

"One last thing," our teacher announced. "Since many of you will be flying on planes today, you'll have an excellent chance to watch the sky. We in the UFO Society have observed a

HErE, SpOt!
Good boy!

great increase in spaceship activity lately. If you see anything, please call 1-888-UFO-SPOT."

Mr. Slomin also happened to be the president of the Clearview UFO Society. He stayed up all night every night, peering into his telescope for spaceships, and phoning to warn the Air Force. Luckily, the Air Force thought Mr. Slomin was a crackpot.

"Well," he told the driver, "it's time to go."

The doors of the school bus folded shut. Through the tinted windshield, I caught a panicked look from Stan. What were we going to do?

Chapter 3
THE OUT·OF·TOWNERS

"*W*a-a-a-ait!*" came a voice behind us.

Everybody wheeled around. A long silver stretch limo screeched into the parking lot.

"Stanley! Don't go! It's me—Mom!"

I let out a long breath. Crfrdnys had come through! We were saved!

A uniformed chauffeur got out and opened the passenger door. Out stepped Stan's "mother." I gawked. Everybody did. Mr. Slomin nearly swallowed his whistle.

It was supermodel Cindy Crawford!

I thought the bus would tip over from everyone rushing to one side to stare at Cindy Crawford. The kids on the lawn burst into applause. The goggle-eyed bus driver let Stan out.

"You mean Cindy Crawford is an *alien*?" I whispered incredulously.

Stan shrugged. "You didn't think a mere Earthling could look like that, did you?"

"Wow," I said. "I never knew you Pants were such an attractive species."

"It's simple technology," Stan explained in a low voice. "Before a big fashion show or photo shoot, Crfrdnys programs her nasal processor to make her extra-gorgeous."

I'd better explain how all this was even possible. When Pants come to Earth, they pose as normal humans. But since they have nose

computers, they're so fantastic at their Earth jobs that a lot of them become famous. Other Pants living on Earth include Michael Jordan, Mark McGwire, Leonardo DiCaprio, Regis Philbin, and two of the four Teletubbies.

Tanner was bug-eyed. "How can Cindy Crawford be your *mother?*" he asked Stan. "You don't even have the same name!"

Or thE SaME MOLE!

"Oh, my real name is Cindy Mflxnys," Crfrdnys explained. "I go by Crawford professionally. All the big modeling agencies are looking for girls with vowels in their last names."

Calista sidled up to Stan. "Do you think you could get your mom to give me an autograph?" she whispered.

"I, Stan, will try."

"Me, too!" added Joey. "Thanks, buddy!"

"No fair!" I exploded. "Five minutes ago everybody was making nose-picking jokes! Now you all act like Stan's best friends just because you found out his mom's famous!"

Mr. Slomin handed Cindy a piece of paper and a pen. "It's for my nephew," he gushed. "I'm—I mean, he's your *biggest* fan. Make it out 'To my favorite teacher, love and kisses, Cindy.'"

"Of course," she said, handing him the autograph. "Now I need a favor from you. I have some photo shoots coming up in Paris, Tokyo, and Neptune—"

"Neptune?" repeated the teacher.

"Neptune, *Vermont*," I put in quickly. "Big modeling community. Lots of photographers."

"So I can't be at home to take care of Stanley," Cindy went on. "Would it be possible for him to stay here a few more weeks?" She fixed her supermodel eyes on our teacher. "Please, pretty please, do this little favor for me?"

Mr. Slomin was the toughest teacher in school. He would stand up to Cindy Crawford. Heck, he would stand up to Godzilla! I held my breath.

"Of course, of course!" Then he added with a sneaky smile, "I'd be happy to keep an eye on that son of yours a little while longer."

So *that's* what our teacher was up to. Mr. Slomin didn't know Stan's true identity. But he had always suspected that there was some

connection between my exchange buddy and his
UFO sightings.

After the bus left, Cindy stuck around to be
"Class Mom" for the rest of the day.
Then her chauffeur drove us home. I
thought up a new rule of coolness on the
spot: **Limos rock!** Man, this was the life!

Whoa, Mama!

"Excellent work, Agent Crfrdnys," Stan was
saying. "I, Stan, am grateful. Now you merely
have to convince Devin's family to let me stay."

The supermodel stuck her finger up her nose to fix her makeup. "Understood, Agent Mflxnys. Are they reasonable life forms?"

"Not really," Stan admitted. "But they have an Earth dog named Fungus who is very pleasant to talk to. He has a terrific sense of humor."

Nasal processors have something called a Pan-Tran translator, which allows Pants to speak any language, including Dog. According to Stan, Fungus was a regular laugh riot. I had to take his word for it, of course. To me, Fungus was the only member of our family who drank out of the toilet. If that little habit showed wit and intelligence, I just didn't get it.

I was kind of hoping that some of the neighbors would be out to see us pull up in a limo, but the block was deserted. Didn't it figure? There were always plenty of spectators on hand when Stan was drilling for oil up his schnoz. But now that we had something cool going on, no one was around.

I let Stan and Cindy into the house ahead of me. "Mom!" I called. "Guess what? Stan has company from—uh—out of town!"

"I know," came my mother's voice from the living room.

"You *know*?" How could she know? **Did they report on CNN that Cindy Crawford is the mother of a notorious nose picker?**

"I'm in here with Stan's uncles right now," Mom called.

"Not his uncles, his *mother*!" I exclaimed.

I stopped short. Side by side on the couch, each drinking a cup of tea and chewing on a paper napkin, sat a pair of Pants named Zgrbnys the Extremely Wise and Gthrmnys the Utterly Clever. We had told my parents they were Stan's uncles Zack and Gus, but they were really Stan's bosses from Pan. If they were here, that meant something was up. Something big!

DiDN'T I TELL YOU TO KEEP YOUR PaNTS OFF THE COUCH!

Chapter 4

CUFFS WILL ROLL

Zgrbnys and Gthrmnys were members of a renowned group of supergeniuses known as the Smarty-Pants. Only the Grand Pant and his assistants, the Under-Pants, are more respected on Pan. To be a Smarty-Pant, you need an IQ so large that even you can't count that high. Stan once showed me a copy of the final exam at Smarty-Pants University. I would have flunked in a heartbeat. You have to recite the infinity times table, take apart a spaceship engine in minus one second, and figure out a way to move a class-A pulsar using nothing but duct tape, paper clips, and a number-two pencil.

"Hi, Uncle Zack! Hi, Uncle Gus!" I exclaimed, winking at the two Smarty-Pants. "Guess who's

here—Stan's mom! Your *sister!*"

"I have no sister," frowned Zgrbnys.

"And neither have I," added Gthrmnys.

I rolled my eyes. For a couple of geniuses, these guys could be thick as bricks.

"I, Stan, can explain—" my exchange buddy began.

But Cindy saved the day. "I'm actually their sister-in-*law*. Stanley's father—my husband—is their brother."

That's when Mom got her first look at Agent Crfrdnys. I thought her eyes would pop out of her head. *"Cindy Crawford!"* she cried. Then, to Stan, *"She's your mother?"*

Luckily, my family was so blown away at finding a supermodel in the house that Stan got the okay to stay as long as he wanted. They liked him anyway. In spite of his dweebiness, he was a really great guy. My parents were convinced he was a positive influence on me. Ever since he'd arrived, my room was clean, the leaves were raked, and all my household chores were done to perfection. Of course, Mom and Dad had no way of knowing it was all the work of an alien schnoz.

"I can't believe they bought it," I whispered to my exchange buddy. "Not one person has raised a single doubt that you're Cindy Crawford's son. Not even Roscoe."

My older brother gave me a hard time about everything. But today he was following Cindy around like her private butler, opening doors for her, and offering her stuff to eat and drink. He practically broke his neck climbing up on two

20

chairs to get Mom's silver tray for her snack. It was pretty funny, because all he could find to put on it was a handful of stale Fritos.

"Since they can see no other reason why a famous model should be in their home," Stan concluded, "they must accept our fabricated explanation."

He had a point. Our story was pretty far-fetched. But could you imagine trying to explain who Cindy *really* was? ☛ **Rule 37:** Never resort to the truth when a good lie can save your bacon.

Dinner was a little wacky that night. Fungus, our cocker spaniel, spent the whole meal telling knock-knock jokes and doing his famous impersonation of the Grand Pant speaking Dog. This had Cindy and Stan howling with hysterics, but naturally, we humans only heard a lot of barking and laughing.

WHO NEEDS TV?

The Smarty-Pants didn't get any of the jokes, so Fungus had to do plenty of explaining.

"Bad dog," scolded my little sister, Lindsay. "You shouldn't be so yappy when we've got company."

"That's quite all right," said Zgrbnys, swallowing

21

his napkin and wiping his mouth with his pork chop. "But I still can't understand why the answer to 'Knock, knock' is always 'Who's there?' Why not 'Your antigravity zircon booster is submerged in swamp water,' or 'Please retrofit my alpha phase modulator with banana-peeling capabilities'?"

Why didN't I think of that?

"Or even 'Rigellian armpit bacteria don't wear contact lenses'?" added Gthrmnys.

My dad was cracking up. "Zack, Gus, you slay me."

After dinner, Cindy left for the airport. She had a night flight to Paris for a fashion show. Stan and I went up to my room with the Smarty-Pants.

"Welcome Zgrbnys and Gthrmnys," said Stan. "May the Crease be with you. What's the news from Pan?"

"Not good," Zgrbnys said gravely. "We intercepted a message from the Pan-Pan Travel Bureau complaint department in the Crab Nebula."

"From the Wide Wale himself?" asked Stan, impressed.

Gthrmnys nodded grimly. "We haven't seen so many dissatisfied customers since the Big Dipper sprang a leak during SoupFest. Thousands of unhappy tourists are tearing at their belt loops and demanding their pantaloons back. The Wide Wale has received a snootful of the worst reports possible."

I had to ask. "Bad weather? Lousy food? Seedy hotels?"

"Even worse," said Zgrbnys. **"The nonhaving of fun."**

"That's serious!" exclaimed Stan. "Cuffs will

roll over this! What tourist attraction is creating such terrible problems? Have the lights gone out again on the Galactic Tour so nobody can see the dark matter?"

Zgrbnys shook his head. "The complaints are coming from right here. On Earth."

Chapter 5

WHY DID THE CHICKEN CROSS THE ROAD?

"On *Earth*?" Stan was appalled. "How can any Pant not love Earth? There are so many wonderful things to do here! Haven't they been caught in traffic jams, bitten by mosquitoes, and been forced to go to the dentist?"

> Every tourist's dream!

"Yes, and they've enjoyed those merriments," confirmed Zgrbnys. "Especially having their teeth drilled. But the main reason why Pants came here was for the allergies. And so far, no one has sneezed."

"But Earth has tons of stuff to be allergic to," I protested. "We've got it all—dust, weeds, pollen, mold, and pet hair. We're practically the Disneyland of allergies. If you can't sneeze here, you won't sneeze anywhere!"

Gthrmnys looked down his nose at me. "Your primitive Q-class mind cannot begin to understand the capabilities of Smarty-Pants. We have beamed our nasal processors off an orbiting satellite to scan the entire Earth. No material on this planet will cause an allergic reaction in a Pant."

"Well, how about we give them all a cold then?" I persisted. **"Maybe we could find some sick guy to sneeze on the silverware at the hotel they're staying at."**

"Impractical," said Zgrbnys. "Too many tourists, too few germs."

My exchange buddy was really upset. "But I, Stan, researched this. I looked back as far as the time of Ptlnys the Unbelievably Magnificent, the first Pant ever to reach Earth. He visited what Earthlings call ancient Egypt. According to his journals, he never stopped sneezing for five minutes due to a severe allergy to Nile Delta goldenrod."

"Do you think he could have been lying?" I asked.

The Smarty-Pants looked at me like I had just

accused Santa Claus of Grand Theft Reindeer.

"Devin-shhhh!" Stan scolded me. "You can't disrespect Ptlnys the Unbelievably Magnificent. He's Pan's most revered hero. He invented the nasal processor. He founded the Smarty-Pants. He was even important in Earth history. Who do you think it was who told Alexander the Good, 'If you really want to make your mark, *Good* just doesn't cut it. You're going to have to be *Great*'?"

TONY thE TigEr?

"Sounds like quite a guy," I commented.

Stan nodded. "He might have been even more successful, but he couldn't get around so well. Ptlnys walked with a terrible limp until the day he died. Some say it was from an infected ingrown toenail that would never heal."

"How did he get that?" I asked.

My exchange buddy shook his head. "Nobody knows. It's one of the great zippered mysteries of the universe. Like, how did the Sphinx of Egypt lose its nose? Or, why did the chicken cross the road?"

"You mean, to get to the other side?" I asked.

There was a moment of stunned silence, and

then Stan and the Smarty-Pants were locked in a joyous embrace.

"'To get to the other side!'" crowed Gthrmnys. "That's brilliant! It completely illuminates the chicken's motivation!"

"This is the first zippered mystery revealed since that glorious day when all Pantkind came to realize why manhole covers are round!" Zgrbnys added breathlessly. "It'll be the feature story of *Seams to Me* magazine!"

"Hey! *Hey!*" I interrupted. "We're talking about the tourists, remember? What happens if they don't pick up some allergies?"

My exchange buddy hung his head. "The Pan-Pan Travel Bureau will eat my contract and I, Stan, will be fired."

I couldn't believe it. "Over *sneezing*?"

"Over false advertising," Zgrbnys corrected. **"You can't promise sneezation when there's nonsneezation."**

"Customer satisfaction is the most important thing in the travel business," Stan explained. "Why, if the unhappy tourists all E-mail their complaints, they could jam the whole Overall. A single nasal processor can send up to twelve thousand messages per second, Devin. Who knows what might happen next? They might even start a letter-writing campaign. Then the people at the Pan-Pan Travel Bureau would develop heartburn from eating so much hate mail. That would be a public health disaster."

Personally, I couldn't have cared less about a bunch of nose pickers with acid indigestion. I was worried about Stan. "But could you stay here on Earth?"

Stan shook his head sadly. "I, Stan, will be called back to Pan, where I'll be demoted to the bargain basement of the Pan-Pan Travel Bureau. There, I'll take my place on the out-of-fashion slacks rack."

"But I'd never see you again!" I wailed.

"Not true," my exchange buddy said bravely. "I, Stan, will work hard until I achieve the status of travel agent again. This should take no longer than sixty years."

DON'T hold your breath!

"*Sixty years?!*" Stan would be 207 by the time he came back, which was still pretty young for a Pant. I mean, on Pan you can't even vote until you turn 250. But in sixty years, I'd be an old guy who had spent his whole life missing his best friend!

That did it. I couldn't help breaking ☞ **Rule 3: Never panic.** "We've got to scrounge up some sneezing! A sniffle! A chill! Sinusitis! *La grippe!* Allergic rhinitis! A postnasal drip! *Anything!*"

"Impossible, Earthling." Gthrmnys sounded impatient.

"It's not impossible!" I insisted. "That Ptlnys guy was allergic to Nile Delta goldenrod! My dad says you can't kill weeds with an atomic bomb!" Frantically, I yanked a book called *The Ancient World* off the shelf over my desk. "There's a whole chapter on Egypt! It's got to say what happened to the goldenrod!"

I handed the book to Stan, who held it out to the Smarty-Pants. Zgrbnys put his finger in his nose and gave a quarter-twist. A beam of light shot out from his nostril, shining a gleaming square on the table of contents. Suddenly, the pages began to turn, speeding up until they were almost a blur. With a *whoosh*, he was done.

"Ah, fascinating reading," smiled Zgrbnys. "You Earthlings are even more backward than I thought. Imagine building an entire temple out of ancient grease."

"Not grease—*Greece!*" I exploded. "It's a country!"

A very
SLiPPery Land.

Zgrbnys was sarcastic. "Oh, yes. Of course you're right and I'm wrong! After all, you're a mere child on a Q-class planet, and I'm *only* a Smarty-Pant, who can think in six dimensions, seven if you include hyperspace."

"But did you find out what happened to the Nile Delta goldenrod?" Stan asked urgently.

"Oh, that." Zgrbnys dismissed this with a wave of his hand. "That's all gone."

"*What?!*" Stan and I chorused.

"Three thousand years ago," Zgrbnys explained pleasantly, "Pharaoh Wheezinhotep IV developed such a strong allergy to the stuff that he ordered every single goldenrod plant in all of Egypt to be pulled up, placed in a humongous vessel, and sunk to the bottom of the Nile."

"*No-o-o-o-o!!*" I howled in agony.

Chapter 6
BACK IN TIME

"Calm down, Devin," said my exchange buddy soothingly. "We have two of the greatest minds in the galaxy to call upon." He turned to the Smarty-Pants. "Can you use your ultra-intelligence to determine the best course of action?"

"Naturally," said Gthrmnys. "You must travel back in time to the day that you recommended Earth as a possible vacation planet."

"Instead, you will select asteroid B-806 in the Great Slime Nebula of Orion," continued Zgrbnys, "famous for its six-foot cockroaches, electric quicksand, and the only professional hockey league for trees in the galaxy. You will not promise sneezation, or anything more exciting than perhaps getting hit with a slap shot by a forty-foot defenseman named Jacques LaMaple."

Is that ON
PLaNet Syrup?

34

"But I, Stan, love Earth," Stan protested. "And asteroid B-806 is a terrible place for a vacation."

"Hold it, hold everything." I turned to the Smarty-Pants. "Did you just say *travel back in time*?"

Gthrmnys chuckled. "Ah, yes. You Earthlings haven't mastered time travel yet. Along with several other of the simplest achievements of science, such as repealing the law of gravity, harnessing the power of the coleslaw molecule, and spinning gold into straw. How quaintly primitive."

I let that pass. "Well then, what's stopping us from time-traveling to ancient Egypt, picking a load of Nile Delta goldenrod, and bringing it back to make the tourists sneeze?"

You could almost hear the *boing!* as those two so-called geniuses realized that they'd missed something.

"There must be some flaw," Stan said, scratching his head. "Otherwise two Smarty-Pants could not possibly have overlooked such a brilliant plan."

"Naturally," agreed Gthrmnys, his finger up his nose. "The flaw is—uh-uh . . ." His voice trailed off.

"The flaw is that there *is* no flaw," concluded Zgrbnys. "And since there's no such thing as a completely flawless plan, there obviously must be a *hidden* flaw. But I wouldn't expect a non-genius to understand."

I was exasperated. "Listen, nobody cares that you didn't think of it! How do we *do* it?"

"Nothing could be simpler," said Zgrbnys. "When high speed and gravity come together, a time warp is created. For example, by flying a tight orbit around your sun, our spaceship would go back in time approximately four minutes."

"Four minutes?" I repeated. "That won't do any good! We need to go three thousand years!"

"In that case, we would merely circle the sun several times," said Gthrmnys. "Three hundred ninety-four million, four hundred seventy thousand times, to be exact."

I'M gETTiNg dizzY juST thiNKiNg abOUt it.

"Allowing for leap years," Zgrbnys added smugly.

"Wow," I said. "You guys have really thought this out."

"That's our job," nodded Gthrmnys. "We're thinkers. **That's why we get paid the plus-size pantaloons.**"

An excited Stan was already herding us out of my room. "Let's get to the spaceship!"

"Hold it," I said. "You think my folks are going to let me fly off to ancient Egypt on a school night? What am I supposed to tell them?"

"Nothing, Earthling," snickered Zgrbnys. "Since we are traveling to the *past*, everything we do there will take no time in the *present*, since it will already have happened thousands of years *before*."

"Then we simply return to this exact moment,"

finished Gthrmnys. "To your parents' eyes, you will walk out, and then immediately walk back in."

"Is that too complicated for the simplicity of your Q-class brain?" added Zgrbnys in genuine concern.

"At least I understand knock-knock jokes," I muttered under my breath. "And so do most kindergarten kids."

We tiptoed downstairs. As a cover, I bagged up the kitchen trash, called, "Mom, I'm taking out the garbage," and slipped through the front door.

On the porch, I glared at Stan and the Smarty-Pants. "This had better work. Otherwise it's going to say on my tombstone that my last words were, 'I'm taking out the garbage.' Now, where's your spaceship?"

The two geniuses looked completely mystified.

"Oh, come on!" I blew up. "You forgot where you left it?"

Gthrmnys was annoyed. "This is top security, Earthling. We conceived of a hiding place so ideal that not even we could find it."

"Dazzling logic!" Stan marveled.

"It was my idea," Zgrbnys said modestly.

"No, it was *my* idea," argued Gthrmnys.

I pointed. "Hey, isn't that your spaceship over there?"

It was at a parking meter on Main Street—a Button-Fly 501 space cruiser from the first fleet

of His Most Tailored Majesty, the Grand Pant. It was shallow and eight-sided, like a giant stop sign, but with a long shiny pipe sticking straight up on top. To be honest, it looked pretty ridiculous in the middle of a line of cars.

"That's your brilliant hiding place? *That?!*" I was furious. "A nearsighted baboon couldn't miss it! If Mr. Slomin had driven by here, he would have called the Air Force on us in a second!"

"It's the perfect spot," argued Zgrbnys. "No one in his right mind would search for an alien spacecraft in the middle of the street. Therefore, that is exactly the correct place to hide it."

Brilliant! "As you can see, nobody noticed it," added Gthrmnys as we approached the spaceship.

"Oh, yeah?" I reached under one of the sixteen windshield wipers and pulled out a small piece of paper. "You two geniuses got a parking ticket—thirty bucks for an expired meter!"

Zgrbnys plucked it from my hand. "We don't have to pay this." He tossed it over his shoulder.

"But the Grand Pant honors all traffic citations," Stan reminded him. "From anywhere in the Milky Way galaxy."

"That's the advantage of a superior intelligence," smirked Gthrmnys. "I have used my limitless brainpower to determine that there's no possible chance that word of this could ever get back to the Grand Pant."

Zgrbnys stuck his finger in his nose. Instantly, the spaceship lifted up off the road and hovered above the cars. A tiny dot appeared in the side. It grew larger, yawning open into a round door. A silver staircase descended to the street, and a red carpet unfurled along it.

I'd seen this before, but it still blew me away. Pants can be pretty goofy, with their fingers up their noses, and all that Big Zipper stuff. But their technology is nothing short of spectacular. They are ahead of Earth in every way. They just happen to be very weird.

No . . .

Stan followed the Smarty-Pants up the stairs. "Come on, Devin," he called down to me. **"This is an emergency. More tourists are *not* sneezing every minute."**

I picked the parking ticket up off the pavement and jammed it in my pocket—I couldn't risk having the police trace it back to my family. Then I ran up the stairs into the spaceship and into the unknown.

Chapter 7
SPITTOON

Takeoff in a Button-Fly 501 space cruiser is like falling from a skyscraper in reverse. One second you're on the ground, totally stopped. The next, you're ten miles high, and the town below you seems like a sprinkling of tiny Monopoly houses. What else is down there? Oh, yeah. Your stomach. I'll bet you never get used to it, even if you do it every day.

DO THEY PUT barf bags ON THOSE SPACEShips?

A moment later, we were so far away that the whole planet looked about the size of a golf ball.

"Unbelievable," I breathed.

"Yes," agreed Stan. "Since the sun is only ninety-three million miles away, we must use extra-slow speed so we don't overshoot our target."

It sure didn't feel very extra-slow to my stomach and me.

"Now," he went on, "I, Stan, have to warn you about SPITTOON."

I gave him a blank stare. "Spittoon? You mean those funky ashtrays cowboys spit chewing tobacco into?"

"SPITTOON stands for Special Priority Intergalactic Time Travel Orders On Noninterference," he explained. "When you visit the past, you must be very careful not to do anything that might change the future."

"How can anybody do that?" I scoffed.

"It's no laughing matter," Stan said gravely. "Time travel can present a very serious problem. For example, what if, by accident, our spaceship lands on somebody? If that person's destiny was to become a great hero, or king, or president, that wouldn't happen, since he would be dead. So the future would change because he would no longer be in it."

I still didn't see what was such a big deal. "So we'll remind the Dummy-Pants to watch where they park the flying saucer."

"I heard that," called Zgrbnys from the controls.

"It's not so simple, Devin," Stan insisted. "Even something as tiny as stepping on an ant can affect the future. That ant might have been just about to bite an evil inventor. If his foot had become swollen, the inventor would have had to stay home from his lab. But he didn't, since the ant never lived to bite him. And that day, the inventor might create a terrible weapon that never should have existed." He was deadly serious. "So time travelers must be sure not to change even the slightest detail when they're in the past."

"We'll just get our goldenrod, pack up, and leave," I promised.

"Entering solar orbit in five seconds," called Gthrmnys. "Four—three—"

We were streaking in toward the sun, closer and closer until the entire view screen was white-hot fire. Solar flares reached for us with exploding fingers of flame. I was positive we would plunge inside and be roasted.

"Hit the brakes!" I howled.

The Smarty-Pants ignored me. "Hang on to

your belt loops!" cried Zgrbnys from the controls. "We're jumping to time-warp speed!"

I felt like a tiny pebble inside the tire of a race car that's driving two hundred miles per hour. The spinning action whipped me up against the wall. Going that fast, it's tough to see; everything is enveloped in a bright white haze. My lips went numb, followed by my fingers and toes. There was a churning in my stomach as if someone had taken a jackhammer to my belly button from the inside. I tried to scream, but the muscles in my jaw wouldn't move.

And just as suddenly, it was all over. With nothing pinning me to the wall anymore, I

collapsed to the floor. Slowly, my vision cleared, and I stared at the view screen. There, dead center, hung Earth.

"Aw, come on!" I exploded. "After all that, we just went *home*?"

"This isn't home, Earthling," Gthrmnys informed me as we started to descend through the atmosphere. **"We have completed approximately four hundred million solar orbits at one hundred million times the speed of light."**

"Yes, this is Earth," added Zgrbnys. "But it's hardly the Earth you know. The year is 1000 B.C."

Stan jumped up, eyes wide. "Then we did it," he said excitedly. "We're in the past."

"Nile Delta goldenrod, here we come!" I cheered. "Hey, what does that stuff look like, anyway?"

Gthrmnys was as blank as a movie screen with the projector switched off. His partner was even blanker, if that was possible.

I wheeled to face Stan. My exchange buddy didn't have a clue either.

I blew my stack. "You mean we just traveled three thousand years into the past, and nobody bothered to find out what we're searching for?"

There was an embarrassed silence. On the view screen, the northeast corner of Africa was hurtling up to meet us.

"Well," suggested Zgrbnys, "after we land, maybe we can find another book—"

"Books won't be invented for two thousand five hundred years," Stan reminded him gently.

"Oh, right," Zgrbnys said lamely. "I forgot."

I seethed all the way down to Earth. I know ☛ **Rule 26** says: What's done is done; don't be a baby about it. But I was really sore.

I was still muttering under my breath when the space cruiser touched down. I slapped my fist into my palm. "Darn it, there must be some way to recognize Nile Delta goldenrod!"

The tiny dot spiraled out into a door. A stiff breeze of hot, dry air blew into the ship. And sud-

PUT SOME NAME TAGS ON THOSE WEEDS!

denly, all four of us were sneezing our heads off!

Chapter 8

THE NOT·SO·GREAT PYRAMIDS

My three companions were overjoyed. There's nothing a Pant likes more than sneezing through his nasal processor. According to Stan, every single one of your trillion gigabytes tingles. He says no earthling feeling could ever be so awesome.

"*Sneezation!*" howled Zgrbnys. "This is—*achoo!*—fantastic!"

"I, Stan—*achoo!*—told you it was worth coming to—*achoo!*—Earth for!"

"It sure beats—*achoo!*—thinking all day!" added Gthrmnys.

"But what's—*achoo!*—causing it?"

I was sneezing so hard I couldn't stay upright.

"It—*achoo!*—must be—" Finally I managed

to crawl to the door and get a look outside. I'll bet my eyes bulged just like in cartoons. *"Nile Delta goldenrod!!"*

It had to be! We were in the middle of a vast field of the stuff—two-foot-high weeds with small yellow spiky flowers. It went on as far as the eye could see in all directions. "Boys," I wheezed happily, "we just hit the goldenrod jackpot."

Stan came up behind me. "There's enough here for every tourist on Earth," he gasped, and then collapsed to the floor sneezing.

We headed down the red carpet. In the middle of the field, the sneezing got even worse, complete with runny nose and itchy, watery eyes. The three Pants rolled around the goldenrod, loving every minute.

I was getting annoyed. I mean, fun is fun, but we were here to save Stan's career. I suppressed another sneeze. "Come on, we've got work to do. Can't you guys take some allergy medicine?"

Zgrbnys looked at me. "Allergy medicine?"

"So you'll stop sneezing!"

"*Stop* sneezing?" Stan repeated, as if I had just suggested they should cut their own throats. "Devin, Pants are willing to travel trillions of miles and spend thousands of hard-earned pantaloons just to *start* sneezing! Why should we do anything to make us—*achoo!*—stop?"

It became so impossible to do anything outside that we had to go back into the ship and seal the door so we could talk about our plan.

I took charge. "Okay, let's start yanking up

goldenrod. It shouldn't take very long for three nose computers to pick a bunch of weeds."

"Devin," Stan said patiently, "a nasal processor could never harvest goldenrod."

"Sure it could," I countered. "It cuts the lawn, right? Why can't it do the same with this stuff?"

"When I use my nasal processor to cut the grass," Stan explained, "it automatically transports all the clippings to Dimension X. But we *need* these goldenrod clippings. And we especially need the seeds. I, Stan, will keep a warehouse in an orbiting satellite. This will automatically reseed the planet whenever the Earthlings get out the weed killer." He turned to the two Smarty-Pants. "Earthlings don't like sneezation."

TEACHER, MY HOMEWORK IS IN DIMENSION X.

"Primitive," muttered Gthrmnys under his breath.

"You mean—" I was horrified. "—you mean we have to pick this stuff *by hand*?"

"Exactly," confirmed Gthrmnys. He turned to his partner. "Feel like doing some sight-seeing?"

"Don't I always?" grinned Zgrbnys.

I couldn't believe it. "You mean you're not even going to *help*?"

"We're thinkers," Gthrmnys chuckled. "Laborious tasks are best left to the doers." He activated the ship's main screen and began flipping around different views of the area, humming under his breath. "Now, what looks interesting? Ah!"

My jaw dropped. "Those are the Great

Pyramids! We learned about them in social studies!"

I was thunderstruck. The ancient wonders looked brand-new. Come to think of it, they *were* brand-new—*now*. The biggest one wasn't even finished yet. As we watched, an army of Egyptian laborers and engineers worked ropes and pulleys to maneuver the top stone into place.

Gthrmnys made a face. "Good heavens, they certainly botched that job."

"Are you nuts?" I howled. "It's totally perfect!"

"That shows what you know, Earthling," Zgrbnys sneered. "It is a full three sixty-fifths of a millimeter off to the left. I'm amazed the whole thing doesn't come crashing down."

PICKY! PICKY!

I was really mad. "The pyramids are one of the most spectacular achievements of the human race."

"Devin," Stan chided gently, "you don't really believe the *Egyptians* built the pyramids, do you?"

"Of course they did. They're doing it right now. Look."

Stan shook his head. "The Great Pyramids were designed by Ptlnys the Unbelievably Magnificent while he was here on Earth. He was the chief engineer on the entire project."

"That's impossible!" I snapped. "And it doesn't make sense. Why would an alien need to build three humongous stone triangles in the middle of nowhere?"

"Ptlnys hadn't invented the nasal processor yet," Stan explained. "So he had no way to communicate with Pan. The pyramids were a message. When viewed from a spaceship, they spell out, 'Arrived safely. Wish you were here,' in Pant shorthand."

That's what I call using big words!

"Let's get over there!" Zgrbnys said excitedly. "Maybe someone will introduce us to Ptlnys the Unbelievably Magnificent!" And they opened the door and rushed out into the goldenrod, sneezing and bickering over who should be first to shake hands with the great Pant hero.

I turned on Stan. "How come you didn't give *them* the lecture on SPITTOON?" I demanded. "Aren't you worried that those two idiots will mess up the future?"

"Devin, they're Smarty-Pants," he scolded me. "They can move a pulsar with duct tape. Every step they take, their superbrains will be guarding against changing history. Trust me."

With the Smarty-Pants off playing tourist, we the "doers" got down to work. I won't try to sugarcoat it. Picking goldenrod is total slavery. Backaches, muscle aches, blisters, not to mention sunburn—when Mr. Slomin taught us about ancient Egypt, he never mentioned it was a hundred and ten degrees in the shade. Painful, exhausting, torturous—to those adjectives, I have to add just one more: *gross*. It's not much fun to have a runny nose thirty centuries before the invention of Kleenex.

After four mind-numbing, backbreaking, sweat-drenched, sneezing, wheezing hours, I finally stuffed the last armload of goldenrod into the hold. Stan tweaked his nasal processor, and the cargo door spiraled shut and winked out of existence.

The two of us collapsed to the ground, totally exhausted. I checked my watch. It was two-fifteen—but I couldn't be sure if that was in Egypt or in Clearview, 1000 B.C., or A.D. 2000 What it did mean was that the Smarty-Pants had been gone for four and a half hours.

"Oh, great," I moaned. "Two morons wandering around ancient Egypt. If somebody busts the Nile, we'll know who to blame."

"Smarty-Pants don't 'wander,' " my exchange buddy lectured me. "They follow carefully calculated paths decided by the supreme logic of their superbrains. I, Stan, am sure they'll be back soon."

But at sundown there was still no sign of the Smarty-Pants.

Chapter 9
MUM'S THE WORD

"Where are they? Where are they? *Where are they?*" I was freaking out.

By this time, even Stan was frowning. "They must have discovered a monumentally important task. They're too busy to check their nasal processors. I've put four APBs out."

"Can't you buzz them directly?" I nagged.

"Well, no," he replied. "Not if they've hung out the *Do Not Disturb* signs on their virtual nose knobs. They're probably doing research that will change our view of ancient Earth. Or they could be repairing some damage to history in keeping with SPITTOON—"

"Or those two boneheads got themselves lost and now they're wandering in the desert somewhere," I suggested.

"We can't wait around to find out," Stan decided. "The longer we stay here, the longer we risk that our ship will be spotted. We could never explain it to the Egyptians without affecting history."

"But what can we do?" I asked. "Our pilots are gone!"

"I, Stan, took Introduction to Flying, part 1 before I flunked out of Smarty-Pants University."

> Just what I always wanted: a ride with a failed pilot.

"You mean," I was thunderstruck, "we're just going to leave them *stranded*?"

"Of course not," Stan replied. "We'll go back to the future and distribute our goldenrod among my fellow travel agents on Earth. Then we'll return here to pick them up."

"And you know where 'here' is?" I sure didn't.

"It's programmed into the navigational computer," Stan assured me as we climbed back into the ship.

When the door sealed, we stopped sneezing. But we were still a mess, with watery eyes and runny noses. So while Stan got us out of first

Egypt and then Earth's atmosphere, I scoured the space cruiser for some Kleenex. There was none in any of the supply closets. But I opened up a drawer marked "Snack Foods" and found ten boxes.

AND LOOK FOR NEW, IMPROVED NACHO CHEESE KLEENEX IN YOUR GROCER'S FREEEZER.

"Oh, delicious," said Stan at the controls, stuffing a handful of tissues in his mouth. He burped. "No more, thank you, Devin. I, Stan, wouldn't want to eat too much and get sleepy while I'm flying."

In answer, I blew my nose so hard I'm amazed I didn't blast a hole in the side of the space cruiser.

I couldn't tell if Stan was a great pilot or not. I still got slammed up against the wall when we whipped around the sun. But he had one really good idea. To avoid being seen, he set us down in a small clearing in the woods at the end of my street.

"Not bad," I commented as we walked down the staircase and headed for home. "What grade did you get in that flying course, anyway?"

"K-minus," he replied.

Top of the class? Low average? Total flunk-out? Anybody's guess is as good as mine.

We stepped out of the clearing and stopped dead. I goggled. I gagged. I did a reality check and never even came close to anything real.

Our house was there, all right. But in a way, it wasn't. Oh, there was the same white wooden siding with green trim, but it wasn't a two-story square anymore. It was a *pyramid*! My horrified eyes moved to the faded blue and a little bit rusty vehicle in the driveway. It wasn't our Honda. It was a motorized four-wheel *chariot*! The blue spruce on the front lawn, the old oak with the tree house, the lilac bushes close to the porch-they were gone. Instead, tall papyrus plants towered everywhere.

I looked around. All the other houses were pyramids, too. The streetlights were shaped like scarab beetles. The fire hydrants were miniature mummies. I blinked a few times, but when my eyes opened again, all that *stuff* was still there.

NOW ENTERING thE TWiLight ZONE!

My brother Roscoe stepped out the door. He was wearing a dress! Well, not a lady's dress, but some kind of tunic. In place of his usual baseball

62

cap was an Egyptian headpiece. **"Hey, guys! Want to play Hounds and Jackals?"** He squinted at us. "What's with the weird outfits?"

"Is it by any chance . . . *Halloween*?" Stan asked hopefully.

"No!" I snapped. "But even if it was, you don't dress up your *house* to go trick-or-treating!"

Stan put his finger in his nose. "Location: Clearview, Earth. Time: A.D. 2000 Life form: Earthling, Roscoe Hunter, age thirteen-point-two."

"That's right!" I hissed. "So why is everything *wrong*?"

"Insufficient data," Stan informed me. But he looked worried.

Things went from bad to worse. My mother turned out to be a priestess of the Nile. Instead of Barbies, my little sister Lindsay played with Nefertiti dolls. My dad worked for a company called Mum's The Word. They manufactured an automatic wrapping machine for mummies. There wasn't much demand for that in the Clearview I remembered. But he told us business was booming.

Our TV was pyramid-shaped, so the picture was a triangle. It would be pretty lousy for watching football. You'd never see any touchdowns since neither end zone would fit on the screen.

I shouldn't have worried. There *was* no football. Instead, we watched *Monday Night Crocodile Wrestling*, *Alexandria Hills 90210*, *Everybody Loves Ramses*, and *Battle of the Monster Chariots*.

DON'T bE a cOUch papyrus!

"Pssst," whispered Stan. "Was TV always like this?"

"Of course not!" I seethed at him.

The crowning moment of the evening came when Pharaoh Tutankhamen the 53rd give his State of the Empire speech. I've never seen a hat that big in my life!

"My fellow Egyptians . . ." he began.

Lindsay pointed to the doorway. "Here comes Fungus."

Fungus! Well, at least one thing was normal. "Come on, Fungus," I beckoned. "Here, boy."

Into the den slithered a small black poisonous snake.

Chapter 10
FREAK SHOW

I hit the ceiling. "Hide! Get a rake! Kill it! Call the cops!"

My mother chuckled. "Very funny, Devin. Fungus has only been our pet asp for five years."

"Pet *asp*?!"

"Of course," she replied. **"Asps are man's best friend."**

"No, they aren't!" I squawked. "Dogs are!"

"*Dogs*? Dogs are wild animals running around the hills in packs. They could never be domesticated."

"Have you all gone crazy?" I yowled. "Dogs make perfect pets. A disgusting viper like that could never do what dogs do!"

"Hey, look," chuckled Roscoe, pointing at the

open bathroom door. "Fungus is drinking out of the toilet again."

I stood corrected.

The asp slithered back into the den and wrapped himself around Stan's ankle. He stuck out a forked tongue and hissed. Stan hissed back.

"He's a pretty nice guy," Stan told me later that night when we were alone in my room. "He doesn't have a great sense of humor like Fungus the dog. But, as asps go, he's quite pleasant."

EVERY SNAKE has his day.

"I don't want a pleasant asp," I complained. "I don't want *any* asp! I want my dog back. What happened to my life?"

"I, Stan, am also confused. It seems the entire world has become a modern version of ancient Egypt. However, my nasal processor indicates that the rest of the galaxy is completely normal, even the planet Pinkus, which is almost never normal. It's just Earth that is, as you say, screwy."

"But how?" I wailed.

"There is only one possible explanation," said Stan, very pale. "We must have committed a SPITTOON violation. Somehow, we changed history when we were in ancient Egypt."

"No chance," I said firmly. "We barely left the spaceship the whole time—" And then it hit me. "The Dummy-Pants!"

"Oh, no, Devin," Stan said firmly. "That could never happen to Smarty-Pants. They're far too intelligent."

"There's only one thing to do," I decided. "We've got to go back to ancient Egypt and fix whatever went wrong."

Stan made a pained face. "Time travel is so tricky. We might even make things worse. Are you sure you can't get used to *this* Earth? Asps aren't so bad, you know. **They can't fetch sticks, but they can impersonate them.** And they're wonderful at discouraging burglars. My nasal processor says that robberies have dropped down to zero in this society because every house is protected by an asp."

"I hope you're joking, Mflxnys," I growled. I lay back in my "bed," which was a mummy case propped against the angled pyramid wall. "Man, there's no way I'll ever sleep in this! It's a coffin! What do they think I am, a vampire? Let's go back to ancient Egypt before bedtime."

YOU'LL SLEEP LIKE THE dead!

"That would be unwise," my exchange buddy said seriously. "Until we know exactly what the damage to history is, it will be difficult to fix it."

"Can't your nose computer figure it out?" I asked.

Stan shook his head. "This is Earth history. My nasal processor can only get information about Pan. We'll need to learn more before we can risk time traveling again."

What a lousy night! My bed gave me nightmares. I couldn't take my eyes off a grotesque

stuffed animal with a person's body attached to the head of a hawk. My mother assured me it was my favorite toy as a toddler. I must have been some little sicko in this world.

Stan, of course, slept like a baby, snoring the microwave-oven hum of his nasal processor. Sure—it wasn't *his* planet that had turned into a freak show.

The next morning, I went through the Egyptian clothes in my closet to find something to wear to Pharaoh Akhenaton the 106th Academy—

formerly Clearview Elementary School. I finally picked out a tunic with gold-leaf stripes from Papyrus Republic. Luckily, there weren't any rules of coolness against guys wearing miniskirts— who could have imagined it would ever happen?

Stan chose a white tunic with a black-and-white polka-dot tie. You can stop history, but you can't stop Stan Mflxnys from being a dweeb.

I thought I looked pretty cool in an Egyptian kind of way. But when I got to school everybody laughed at me.

"Oh, Devin," giggled Calista. "No one dresses in *chariot-wear* anymore." This from a girl who looked like she was wrapped in the living room drapes.

"I pledge allegiance to the flat stone tablet of the United Empire of Egypt, and to the dictatorship for which it stands. One kingdom under Ra, uninvadable, with chariots and mummification for all."

No kidding, that's how the pledge went. I almost choked when I heard what the other kids were reciting. I was never a big fan of my old school, but today really taught me some appreciation. To start with, our classroom was at the very top of the pyramid. Every time I got up from my desk, I smashed my head against the sloping wall.

I had flunked three tests by 10:30 in the morning because everything was in hieroglyphics. It was all Greek to me—or at least Egyptian. Stan used his Pan-Tran translator to help me. But that meant he had his finger up his nose practically full-time. Nose picking wasn't any more popular in this world than it was in the real one. Mr. Slomin, whose tunic bore the crest of the UFC Society (Unidentified Flying Chariots), sent him to stand out in the hall.

From there, my faithful exchange buddy beamed signals from his nasal processor back into the class to translate my Rules of Coolness notebook, which I found in my desk.

I watched in wonder as the hieroglyphics slowly came apart and rearranged themselves first into letters, and then into words.

Chapter 11

THE CLASS JACKAL

I couldn't believe it. My precious rules were all twisted. ☛ **Rule 15** was supposed to be: Never wear white after Labor Day. Now it was: Never wear white after the third eclipse past the Festival of Ra.

 And there was some stuff in there that was totally out in left field, like ☛ **Rule 21:** Let sleeping crocodiles lie; ☛ **Rule 34:** A guy's home is his pyramid; and ☛ **Rule 60:** Don't believe everything you read on the obelisk.

It was all downhill from there. At lunch, when I asked for a hot dog, the cafeteria lady didn't know what I was talking about. When I pointed, she scowled, "Why didn't you just say you wanted a 'hot asp'?"

And when I tried to pay with a dollar bill, she made a big stink about it. With a sinking heart, I

looked around. Everybody else's money was brightly colored, with a picture of Pharaoh What's-His-Name on it.

"You're a counterfeiter!" she accused.

By this time, half the school had gathered around to watch me get chewed out.

"It's—Monopoly money!" I stammered. "I stuck it in my tunic instead of back in the game box—"

Eventually, the assistant principal came and ordered me to empty my pockets. He confiscated all my cash—$4.71; not a fortune, but who likes to throw money away? All I got to keep was a few pieces of linty candy, an old comb that looked like it had been used to clean the cooties out of a Sasquatch, and the Smarty-Pants' parking ticket. I also wound up with a week of detentions for trying to pass funny money.

"Don't worry," whispered Stan, "since this is all part of an incorrect future, your detentions aren't technically real."

"So I suppose it was just a dream when the assistant principal was screaming in my face," I mumbled. "He had onions for lunch. Yuck!"

We slipped into Mr. Slomin's room just in time for our Dynastics lesson.

"Today," the teacher was saying, "we're going to learn about the empire we live in."

He pulled a large hanging map down in front of the board. It was a totally normal map of the world, except that there were no borders, and it was all one color. A single word was written in hieroglyphics across the whole thing. I'd learned to recognize it by now. It said: EGYPT.

I raised my hand. "But what happened to all the other countries?"

That got a big laugh.

"Devin, stop being the class jackal," the teacher scolded. "You know perfectly well that Egypt swallowed up all the other countries a long time ago. Ever since Yemen surrendered in A.D. 16. That's why the whole world is Egypt today."

> YOU gOT THE WHOLE WORLD . . . IN ONE COUNTRY . . . .

Suddenly, Stan kicked me hard under the table.

"Ow!"

I glared at him, but he just kicked again.

"Ow!" Then, in a lower voice, "What did you do that for?"

Stan raised his hand. "Mr. Slomin, can we be excused for a few minutes?"

The teacher scowled at him. "Absolutely not, Stan. Dynastics is your second-most important class—after Egyptology, of course."

But my exchange buddy wasn't so easily discouraged. Up went his finger into his left nostril. Instantly, the faucet at the back of the class sprang to life. But instead of running into the sink, the stream of water shot clear across the

room, turned left to avoid Joey Petrillo, and
drenched Stan and me.

Stan removed his finger, and the
faucet shut off.

A NOSE-PICKING
CLAPPER!

"All right, Devin and Stan," ordered Mr.
Slomin. "Go dry yourselves off. And stop in to
ask the custodian to check our sink."

In the hall, I grabbed Stan by his polka-dot tie.
"What's the big idea of turning Niagara Falls on
us?"

"That's it! That's it!"

He was leaping up and down with excitement. If we couldn't fix history, I was going to have to add a new rule of coolness: No jumping in an Egyptian tunic unless you want to show the whole world your underwear.

"That's what?" I asked.

"That's where history got changed," Stan explained. "The *real* Egypt was conquered, but this one went on to take over the entire planet. We must have done something to make ancient Egypt too strong."

"Can we fix it?" I asked nervously.

"We must try," he said somberly. "This is a severe SPITTOON violation. But first—" He put his finger up his nose. Out of the other nostril, an enormous blast of hot air practically knocked me over. In a split second, my sopping wet hair and clothes were completely dry.

"Thanks—I think," I mumbled while my exchange buddy turned the nostril on himself.

I felt kind of uneasy marching out of school in the middle of the day. I reminded myself that this Egyptian school—this whole Egyptian *world*—

was nothing more than a mistake. A mistake that we were on our way to correcting.

A mistake that couldn't be fixed with a red pen . . .

The spaceship was still in the woods where we left it—no tickets or anything like that. Stan took us up and out of the atmosphere. This time I stayed close to the wall. It was a good move. I didn't get bounced around nearly as much when we circled the sun.

Suddenly, the ship lurched. I came off the wall like I'd been shot out of a cannon.

Crack! I bumped heads with Stan, who had been pitched out of the pilot's seat. Through the bright white speed-haze, I could see sparks shooting out of the control panel.

"It's the navigation computer!" Stan cried. "We're losing power!"

"How bad is it?" I shouted back.

"We have to make the ship lighter!" came the reply. "Otherwise, we'll break up and fall into the sun!"

Chapter 12
THE SOLAR SNEEZE

"Fall into the sun?"

I only got a C in science, but that didn't sound too healthy to me. I ran around the ship, looking for heavy things to get rid of. It was no use. All the furniture was bolted down.

"Breakup in ten seconds!" exclaimed Stan. "Nine—Eight—"

Then it came to me. "The cargo bay door! Open it!"

We were bouncing around so badly that it took precious seconds for Stan to find his nostril with his finger.

"Quick!" I howled.

Suddenly, our view screen filled with Nile Delta goldenrod. It seemed like space itself was full of the stuff. It billowed around our ship like a yellow nebula—four agonizing hours of bending, and picking, and cramming! We watched the cloud take on a funnel-shape as gravity began to suck every last seed and flower into the fiery sun.

"We're stabilizing," reported Stan, relieved.

There was a huge disturbance on the solar surface. A colossal flare exploded out like a flaming battering ram. The whole ship shook as it burst past us.

"It *sneezed*!" I exclaimed. "The sun is allergic to Nile Delta goldenrod, too!"

"*Gesundheit,*" said Stan.

His ultrapolite manners could be annoying at times. But somehow, that was exactly the right thing to say.

We headed on to Earth—the ancient one, that is.

I was feeling pretty sour as we began our descent to the Egyptian desert. "I'm *so* not in the mood to start picking goldenrod again. All that work just to have the stuff burn up in the sun. What a waste!" I added, "Then again, if something has to burn, let it be the goldenrod, not us."

Stan set us down in exactly the same spot as the last time. The portal spiraled open, and I felt a blast of that arid desert air. I was halfway out the door before I realized that something was missing. I wasn't sneezing, and neither was Stan.

I looked down. We were supposed to be in the middle of a vast field of knee-high weeds. Instead, there was nothing but sand as far as the eye could see.

"Stan, what happened to all the goldenrod?"

My exchange buddy put his finger in his nose. "Uh-oh. Due to our computer malfunction, we have landed in ancient Egypt five years *later* than last time."

"You mean that Pharaoh Wheezinhotep guy has already gotten rid of it?" I asked, horrified.

"We have bigger problems than that, Devin," Stan said, agitated. "We may have arrived too late to repair the damage done to the past. Aw, twill!"

We had to be in pretty big trouble for Stan to use the T-word. Remember, he's a very polite guy.

Not the T-Word!

"Couldn't we just go back and fly around the sun a few million more times?" I asked hopefully.

"Not until we can repair our navigation computer. Only the Smarty-Pants can do that." He wrung his hands together nervously. "I, Stan, can't imagine how this could be any worse."

"Yoo-hoo," came a voice. "Hello up there."

I looked down. There, waiting for us at the bottom of the stairs, stood a bedraggled, down-on-his-luck Egyptian. Oh, *no*! *This* was how things could be worse! We could never explain our ship and ourselves without breaking the laws of SPITTOON and scrambling the future even more!

"Go away!" I stammered. "We're a mirage! A figment of your imagination! You're seeing things! It's the desert heat!"

The poor old wretch listened patiently to my babbling. Then he said, "May the Crease be with you."

"A *Pant!*" cried Stan in delighted relief.

Chapter 13

THE BIGGEST NOSE PICKER
IN HISTORY

We rushed down to the newcomer.

"I am Agent Mflxnys of the Pan-Pan Travel Bureau," Stan introduced himself. "On Earth I am called Stan. This Earthling is Devin Hunter. He knows the pleated ways of our world."

The ragged Pant said, "My name is Ptlnys."

"Ptlnys the Unbelievably Magnificent!" Stan snapped to a rigid salute, ending with his finger up his nose. "What an honor! I, Stan, feel like a short Pant of seventy again! I must be blushing to the tips of my cuffs!"

Ptlnys seemed confused. "Unbelievably Magnificent? I am not known by this title. I am Ptlnys the Very Average."

EVErybody has to
start SOMEWhErE.

"You may be average now," Stan assured him. "But you will go on to become the greatest hero of all Pant-kind!"

Surely there was some SPITTOON law against telling a guy about his own future. But here was Stan, blabbing away like a kindergarten tattletale.

The famous Pant's eyes narrowed. "How could you know all this?"

Stan spilled what was left of the beans. "We're time travelers from the future."

"Time travel!" exclaimed Ptlnys. "Remarkable! If—" he added, "if it's all true."

I spoke up. "I can prove it."

I pulled the Smarty-Pants' parking ticket out of my tunic and placed it in Ptlnys's dirty hands. "Check out the date—April 16, 2000."

"I'm flabbergasted!" said Ptlnys. "Tell me about the future."

"Which one?" I asked sourly. "There's a really cool one with MTV, NASCAR, and the World Wrestling Federation, but there's also one where you have to watch commercials about crocodile repellent with your pet snake. Now, if you'll excuse us, we've got a really big problem to take care of."

Stan pulled me aside. "Devin," he hissed, "we can't leave him like this!"

"Like what?" I asked. But I knew exactly what he meant. The guy's robes were torn and ratty, and he had no sandals to protect his feet from the hot desert sand. He was dirty and—no offense to Pan and its greatest legend—he smelled pretty bad. "Hey, Ptlnys, how'd you like to come on board our ship and, you know, take a shower or something."

> Stranded thousands of years before the invention of deodorant!

Ptlnys looked surprised. "I am producing odoriferous emanations?"

"You reek," I confirmed as kindly as I could.

"You stop noticing when you live in the desert. Everything smells like sand." He seemed depressed. **"I have become a soiled Pant in need of the Great Dry Cleaner of the universe."**

"How can the designer of the pyramids come upon such hard times?" Stan asked in concern. "You were the master engineer for Pharaoh Wheezinhotep IV."

Ptlnys lowered his eyes. "Alas, great Wheezin-hotep has gone to the House of the Dead," he said mournfully. "In recent years, the new co-Pharaohs have stopped all pyramid-building. Their interests lie more in scarab racing, redecorating the palace in wicker, skinny-dipping in the Nile, and replacing the statues of the gods with balloon animals." He looked disgusted. "I have never met two bigger idiots in my life."

"We are searching for colleagues from the future," my exchange buddy told him. "Would you like to assist us?"

Ptlnys shook his head. "My time on this world is nearly finished. That's why I approached you. I thought your ship had come to take me back to Pan. In the meantime, I've been planning a new project called the nasal processor."

"The nasal processor!!" I thought Stan would launch himself clear on up into orbit.

Ptlnys didn't share his enthusiasm. "It isn't going very well. I don't think it's going to work. I'm considering giving it up."

"No!" cried Stan. "It *will* work! The nasal processor will revolutionize all Pant-kind! And in gratitude, the Grand Pant will promote you to the top drawer and declare you the very first Smarty-Pant!"

Ptlnys brightened. "Would you like to see my sketches for the working model?"

Stan glowed. "There could be no greater honor. Where is your schematic diagram?"

"Turn around," invited the great inventor.

We did. I gawked. There was something new to this area since our last visit. Something *gigantic*.

We followed Ptlnys around to the other side of the mammoth structure.

I nudged Stan. "I thought you said Ptlnys had a really bad limp. This guy walks just fine."

"You're right," Stan confided in a whisper. "Do you think the legend of the Unbelievably Magnificent's ingrown toenail could be false?"

Before I could answer, I got my first look at what Ptlnys was leading us to. I thought my eyes would pop right out of their sockets.

It was the Sphinx—the famous one we had learned about in social studies! It towered over our ship, surveying the desert with blank stone

eyes. But in our millennium, the Sphinx's nose had disappeared over the centuries—even Pants called it a great zippered mystery. Here the thing was almost new, with a schnoz that looked like it should have had a fake mustache and glasses attached to it. And—I gawked—**the Sphinx had one giant carved finger up its massive nostril!**

We were looking at the biggest nose picker in history!

Ptlnys led us up a series of rickety bamboo ladders to the colossal face of this wonder of the ancient world. I was terrified that a weak rung would break, pitching me to my death in the sand hundreds of feet below. But Stan was so psyched he was practically sprinting up the ladders. I remembered ☛ **Rule 22:** Don't be a spoilsport, and climbed on.

There I was, clinging to a piece of bamboo, Ptlnys's smelly feet about three inches from my face. I leaned over to examine the Sphinx's nose. Writing was scribbled all over the smooth surface of the rock—equations, and calculations, and circuit diagrams, not to mention thousands of notes like: LEFT NOSTRIL COMMUNICATIONS ARRAY CONNECT HERE, and NOSE HAIRS MUST BE COMBED AWAY FROM MAIN POWER RECEPTOR and IN CASE OF DEVIATED SEPTUM, PULL NASAL PLUG.

Even I was impressed. Stan was totally blown away.

"Ptlnys," he breathed, "this is fantastic—"

Suddenly, a voice bellowed, "Put your hands up, and step away from the nose!"

Chapter 14
THE CO·PHARAOHS ARE IN

I looked down. A patrol of Egyptian soldiers was gathered at the base of the Sphinx, waving swords and spears at us. Their captain cried, "Congratulations, lads! We've captured the foul scum who have been vandalizing the Sphinx!"

"It's not vandalism!" I called down. "It's—" How would you describe it? Diagrams for a nose computer? Oh, I don't think so.

Did I say it was hard climbing *up* those ladders? Well, try going *down* while being watched by a pack of armed ancient warriors. I noticed Ptlnys sticking the parking ticket in a small pocket in his rags just before they arrested us.

"Ptlnys," sneered the captain as his men shackled us together with heavy chains around our ankles. "I should have known you'd have sour grapes over getting fired from your cushy pyramid-building job."

"The co-Pharaohs are nothing but a couple of papyrus pushers!" Ptlnys said defiantly. "The tallest structure in all Egypt was an anthill before I got here! You tell *that* to your bosses."

The captain uttered a cruel laugh. "You can tell them yourself. The mighty ones want to pass sentence on the Sphinx terrorists personally!"

He ran a critical eye over the Button-Fly 501 Space Cruiser, which stood behind the Sphinx. "What manner of carriage is this? What happened to the horses that pull it?" When no one answered, he said, "Call the tow-chariot. I'm impounding this vehicle in the name of the co-Pharaohs."

With an ominous clang, our chains were attached to the back of one of the chariots. The captain cracked his whip. "To the palace!"

The chariot lurched forward. We were able to run along behind it for about three steps before we fell. Then they dragged us all the way to the capital city of Thebes. You know how you can't spend a day at the seashore without getting sand

in your bathing suit? Well, by the time we reached Thebes, I felt like I had a whole beach in my tunic, complete with shells and soda cans, and about fifty dollars in loose change.

"On your feet, maggots!" ordered the captain. He was a lot like a modern-day drill sergeant.

Dazed and choking, we struggled upright and

tried to brush tons of sand and dust out of our clothes. Before us loomed the great palace, huge and intimidating. Mr. Slomin had taught us about this place in Social Studies. It was designed to make ambassadors return to their home countries and tell their kings, "Don't mess with Egypt." It sure was having that effect on me. I'd never been so scared in my life!

Stan looked nervous too. "Ptlnys," he asked, "do you happen to know the penalty for defacing a public Sphinx?"

"The prisoner is given a choice," Ptlnys explained. **"Death by hanging, death by beheading, death by disemboweling—"**

"I get the picture," I interrupted. "The key word is"—I shuddered—"death. Thanks a lot, Mr. Good News."

"Don't worry," promised Ptlnys. "Before our execution, I intend to give the co-Pharaohs a piece of my mind."

Oh, wow. That would show them. I felt *so* much better now.

"Move!"

I felt a spear-point pressing against my back,

so I started forward. Into the palace they marched us, past glittering rooms filled with treasure, guarded by hundreds of soldiers.

> It's a nice place to visit, but I wouldn't want to be under arrest there!

"Listen, Stan," I whispered. "You know Rule 9?"

He put his finger in his nose. "Never rat out your friends?" He had all my rules of coolness stored on the septum-drive of his nasal processor.

"Right," I confirmed. "Well, delete it. When they bring us to the co-Pharaohs, I'm going to rat Ptlnys out. Remember, neither of *us* wrote on that Sphinx."

Stan was shocked. "Devin! What about SPITTOON? Ptlnys the Unbelievably Magnificent must go on to be the greatest hero in the galaxy."

"Ptlnys is toast either way," I argued. "We can't get dragged down with him. SPITTOON has to protect *us* too! We're not supposed to die in ancient Egypt. Heck, we're not even scheduled to be *born* for thousands of years!"

The guards stopped us at a huge set of golden doors. Out in front stood a tall shirtless guy who didn't have a single speck of hair anywhere on his head, his chest, his arms, or even his eyebrows. His skin gleamed with perfumed oil. He was holding up an ornate scroll with a message written in hieroglyphics.

"What does it say?" I whispered to Stan.

Stan put his finger in his nose to activate his

Pan-Tran translator. "'The co-Pharaohs are in,'" he told me. "If you flip it over, it probably tells you they're out."

Baldy put down the scroll and began to beat deep mournful kabooms on a kettledrum. "You are about to enter the chamber of the twin sons of heaven," he intoned dramatically. "Wielders of the mighty sword of Egypt, brothers to the gods themselves . . ."

The massive doors began to swing open.

"Kneel before the great co-Pharaohs, you maggots!" ordered the captain, aka the drill sergeant.

The guards shoved us to the hard marble floor. When I looked up, I was staring into the faces of the co-Pharaohs themselves.

I'm amazed I didn't have a heart attack right there in front of their wicker thrones.

They were none other than our missing Smarty-Pants, Zgrbnys and Gthrmnys!

YOU're kidding!

Chapter 15
SPIES

The "co-Pharaohs" were snacking on sheets of papyrus and bickering over who would get to wear the crown next. They seemed pretty surprised to see us. After all, Stan and I had dropped them off in the past just yesterday. But to them, five long years had gone by.

"Oh, hello," Zgrbnys said weakly. "Fancy meeting you here."

I can't remember ever being so mad. I scrambled up in a blind rage. "You *idiots*! You stupid, lamebrained *morons*!"

Even Stan couldn't stick up for the Smarty-Pants this time. I mean, I knew they had messed up history. But I always figured it must have been by accident! Forget it! There was nothing accidental about getting yourself put in charge of an empire.

A huge young Egyptian with a jeweled breast-plate not quite hiding a barrel chest turned to the co-Pharaohs. "You know this boy?"

Gthrmnys held the two-piece scepter of Egypt, the crook and flail, in the shape of an X is his lap. "Oh, no, Prince Tutansweet," he replied airily. "Never seen him before in my life."

It was sort of true. I had first run into the Smarty-Pants in A.D. 2000, which wasn't for a long, long time yet.

"Maybe so," I snarled. **"But three thousand years from now you're going to be the stupidest person I ever met in my life!"** I shifted my blistering gaze to Zgrbnys. "In a first-place tie with *you*!"

"Prince Tutansweet is the son of the late Pharaoh Wheezinhotep IV," Zgrbnys explained pleasantly. "He was kind enough to let us have his throne."

What a guy!

He and Gthrmnys sang a rousing chorus of "For He's a Jolly Good Fellow." I guess that's how you thank a guy for letting you be king.

"But—" Stan's voice was full of bewilderment. "—you didn't follow the code of SPITTOON! You were supposed to avoid all contact with Egyptians! Becoming king counts as contact!"

"Well, that's just being nitpicky," said Zgrbnys in a crabby tone.

Ptlnys was dismayed. "You mean the two missing colleagues"—he pointed to the co-Pharaohs—"are *them*?"

I was pretty close to losing it. "But you said you were thinkers, not doers!" I wailed. "If getting crowned Pharaoh isn't *doing*, what is?"

"We're thinkers for our *job*, Earthling," Gthrmnys corrected me. "We can still be doers in our spare time."

"You *numbskulls*—"

Prince Tutansweet held out a meaty palm like a policeman directing traffic. "Be silent, boy." He reminded me of an old-fashioned year 2000 WWF wrestler, one with an Egyptian theme. He sure had the build for it. "The co-Pharaohs are not numbskulls. Nor are they idiots or morons. In fact, the only unpleasant thing about

them is a single bad habit. Alas, the mighty ones engage in nasal excavation."

THEY'rE NASAL ENgINEErs.

Nasal *what*?! "You mean nose picking?"

"We choose to overlook this," the prince went on, "in the case of two such gifted inventors."

"Inventors?" Fat chance! Those two couldn't discover ice in the freezer. And then it began to come together in my head. Inventors . . . nose picking . . .

I turned blazing eyes on the Smarty-Pants. "You've been using your nasal processors to give them stuff, right? Advanced technology from the future. That's why they let you be co-Pharaohs."

Busted!

"It's a filthy lie," proclaimed Zgrbnys. "Oh sure, we may have dropped a few *hints* to help our friends build a few things ahead of time. Like the microwave oven—"

Stan was horrified. "Microwave oven?"

"We needed it to make the low-fat popcorn," added Gthrmnys reasonably. "You can't expect us to be stranded in the past without a few of the necessities of life."

I folded my arms. "What else?"

Zgrbnys blinked. "Well, there's the Mickey Mouse night-light, the Weedwacker, the Chia Pet, the Clapper, and that's pretty much it, you know—unless you want to count the B-52 Strato-fortress bomber."

I choked. **"You gave an *ancient* civilization a B-52?!"**

Gthrmnys shrugged. "There was this rampaging army of Mesopotamian invaders—"

"No wonder Egypt never lost any wars!" I exploded. "It wasn't much of a fair fight! On one side, clubs and arrows! And on the other? A *B-52!*" I rolled my eyes at Stan. "'Oh, they couldn't possibly mess up history,'" I mimicked savagely. "'They're Smarty-Pants?' Well, I've got four words for you, pal: *I told you so!*"

Stan was too shocked to reply.

Prince Tutansweet was wide-eyed. "Are you saying that the mighty co-Pharaohs aren't even real Egyptians?"

Uh-oh. Me and my big mouth.

"Spies!" cried the prince, snatching the crown from Zgrbnys's head. He tried to take the crook and flail away from Gthrmnys, but the stubborn Smarty-Pant wouldn't let go.

"We're loyal Egyptians!" Gthrmnys grunted as the tug-of-war continued, the colorful fly whisk flapping back and forth between them. "Didn't we give you the electric egg-cooker and the Nintendo PlayStation?"

"Guards!" barked the prince.

Ever wonder how many ancient Egyptians it takes to beat up a couple of Smarty-Pants? Six.

Four to hold them down, and two to chain them to Ptlnys, Stan, and me.

Tutansweet set the crown on his own head and sat on one of the wicker thrones. "I, Tutansweet, son of Wheezinhotep, take my rightful place as Pharaoh of Egypt. The names Zgrbnys and Gthrmnys will be carved from the face of every tablet and megalith in the land. So it shall be written; so it shall be done."

"But what about us?" asked Stan.

"As for the foreign spies," the new ruler went on, "including the ex-co-Pharaohs, **I sentence them to be mummified alive and buried under the heaviest pyramid in all Egypt.**"

Ouch!

Suddenly, life with a pet asp didn't seem that bad.

Chapter 16
MUMMIFICATION

Everybody has heard of the three Great Pyramids of Giza. But not a lot of people know about the massive Trump pyramid, which is larger than all the others combined. That was where we were taken to face our punishment for the crime of spying against the Egyptian Empire.

It was a pretty big show, too. In modern times we have baseball fans and hockey fans and horse racing fans. Well, the ancient Egyptians had execution fans. It seemed like the whole country showed up—all except Pharaoh Tutansweet. He found mummifications boring, and stayed home with his Nintendo PlayStation. He was probably whipping up some low-fat popcorn in the microwave, too.

The crowd was cheering like crazy. You would have thought this was the Super Bowl. They even had snack guys selling jackal chips and Croco-Jacks. They were also doing a booming business in T-shirts with a slogan written in hieroglyphics.

"What does it say?" I whispered to Stan.

"'Mom and Dad witnessed a mummification and all I got was this lousy tunic,'" my exchange buddy translated.

"Get your souvenir programs here!" barked another vendor. "You can't tell who's being mummified without a program!"

I know ☛ **Rule 33** says: No groveling. But when I wrote my rules of coolness, I wasn't exactly expecting to get executed. If there ever was a time for groveling, this was it.

"I'm too young to be a mummy!" I pleaded. "I'm not even supposed to be born for three thousand years! Please, *please* don't mummify me!"

The crowd only cheered louder. To an execution fan, watching someone grovel is like getting to see a grand-slam home run.

Do I need to say it? Mummification isn't much fun. First they paint you all over with this disgusting gluey stuff. Next you're wrapped from head to toe with supertight cloth bandages. Then you're placed in a mummy case where all that stuff starts to harden. When I was seven, I broke my arm, and the cast took three days to dry. It was cold and clammy and totally gross. Well, this was twenty times worse because it was all over me.

Once I was wrapped up and shut inside, I couldn't see what was going on. But judging from the roar of the crowd, my fellow prisoners were getting mummified, too. I remember Stan's voice quavering, "I, Stan, regret that I have but one nose to give for the Pan-Pan Travel Bureau." The Smarty-Pants were arguing over who would be a more intelligent mummy. Ptlnys the Unbelievably Magnificent must have gone to his fate in dignified silence, because I never heard a peep from him.

I was aware of my mummy case being lifted up and placed on a horse-drawn cart.

"All right!" bellowed the chief executioner.

"The show's over! Go on home! Nobody's allowed at the burial site!"

There was a loud chorus of boos, followed by sounds of the crowd breaking up. The cart began to roll forward.

"I, Stan, am most sincerely sorry, Devin," came a voice from the mummy case next to mine.

I should have been out of my mind with rage. I should have been cursing the day Stan Mflxnys came rolling out of the baggage chute at the Clearview Airport.

But when I opened my mouth, I had no harsh words for my exchange buddy. "Are you kidding?" I crowed. "Thanks to you, I've seen things most Earthlings only dream about. I barely even knew there was a galaxy out there before you and your magic nose came along. And now I've—"

Hold it! That was the answer! I couldn't believe I hadn't thought of it sooner. There *was* a way out of this mess. It was as plain as the nose on your face! Or at least, the nose on *Stan's* face!

You have to use your head—or your nose.

"Your nose!" I cried. "Stan, can't you use your nasal processor to get us out of here?"

"My nasal processor would be most helpful," Stan replied, "but I, Stan, have no way to reach it. My hands are immobilized."

Uh-oh. Stan needed a finger to work his nose computer. And his arms were tied up across his chest, the same as mine.

"Well, what about the Smarty-Pants, then? Anybody got a free hand?"

"Quiet, Earthling," came Zgrbnys's voice from my left. "I am calculating the amount of air we will have in our mummy cases once we are buried. I estimate three-point-two minutes."

"Not even close," chortled Gthrmnys from the other side of Stan. "The correct number is two-point-nine minutes."

Were there ever such idiots? I guess their pea brains only held one thought at a time. How else could they squabble over how long the air would last without considering what would happen when it ran out?

The carts stopped. I was aware of being lifted up and placed on rough earth. Then I was sliding down what must have been a tunnel. Until that moment I could still sense a little light coming in under the lid of the mummy case. Suddenly, I was in total darkness, so I knew I was under the Great Pyramid. I heard the

sound of shovels working, and then nothing.

Cold panic seized me. I squirmed as if I could break through the tape, the mummy case, and the thousands of tons of pyramid above me.

"Let me out!" I shrieked. There was a ripping sound, and my hand broke through the heavy bandages.

I WANT MY MUMMY!

I pushed the mummy case door open and felt through the loose dirt until my hand reached the casket next to mine. I knocked. "Stan?"

His muffled voice was incredulous. *"Devin?!"*

"I can slip my hand into your coffin." This was a sentence most fourth graders never have a chance to use. "But you're going to have to tell me what to do."

Yes, it was true. In order to get out of this pickle, I would have to break one of my oldest and most precious rules of coolness—the classic

☛ **Rule 5:** You can pick your friends, and you can pick your nose. But you can't pick your friend's nose.

Is he saying what I think he's saying?

Chapter 17
A TICKLISH SITUATION

I wedged my hand inside the opening in his mummy case and patted around. Wouldn't you know it? Stan was ticklish. His taped body trembled. Snickering laughter bubbled out of the mummy case next to me.

"Stop it!" I hissed. "You're wasting air!"

"Sorry," he gasped. "We Pants are a very ticklish species. Our fabric is known to be delicate."

He did his best to hold still. I was able to find his neck. From there it was easy navigation: chin, mouth—jackpot! Carefully, I eased my finger through the sticky tape covering his nose and dug into a nostril.

Eureka!

Was it gross? Disgusting? Nauseating? Repulsive? Amazingly, not at all. There was nothing but machinery up there. It was no different from sticking your finger into the printer port on a computer—only a lot more complicated. There were thousands of tiny buttons, levers, and switches. How was I ever going to figure out the right ones?

A breath caught in my throat, and I choked. We were starting to run out of air!

"I told you it was two-point-nine minutes," said Gthrmnys smugly.

Well, I just started pressing away—anything and everything. If I could feel it against my finger, I hit it. I was puffing now. "How am I doing?" I rasped.

"You just ordered an extra-large pizza with double anchovies to be delivered to the Ring Nebula."

"Stan, I'm not going to make it in time!" I gasped. "The air is getting thinner—"

"Move your finger to the left," Stan ordered briskly. "To the right . . . straight up . . . now in a little half-circle . . ."

I followed his directions word for word. Inside his nose, I could feel buttons pushing, switches flipping, dials turning. And then—

The desert itself trembled as the colossal Trump pyramid lifted itself ten feet straight up off the ground. The sand above us disappeared in a whirlwind.

"Hang on!" cried Stan.

Stan and I, Ptlnys, and the Smarty-Pants were lifted up out of our mummy cases by a force that was both gentle and unstoppable at the same time. Round and round we spun as the bandages flew off us. But my finger never left Stan's nose, like a strong magnet was holding it there.

"How is this *possible*?" cried Ptlnys.

"Behold the power of the nasal processor!" announced Stan.

I could have sworn that his Munchkin voice sounded a little deeper just then.

It was amazing! Stan and I had wriggled out of some tight spots before, but nothing like this. "Mflxnys, I *love* you!" I bellowed. "Put 'er there!" Right there in the shadow of the hovering pyramid, I grabbed his hand and shook it.

For a split second, I couldn't understand the look of pure horror on Stan's face. Then it hit me: my finger was out of his nasal processor.

There was nothing holding up the pyramid anymore!

"Run!" I wailed.

Desperately, the five of us hurled ourselves
away from the falling pyramid.

BOOOOOOOM!! It slammed back down to
the desert with the force of thousands of tons of
solid rock. The impact kicked up a cloud of sand
a quarter-mile high.

"YEEEEEEEE-OWWWWWWWW!!!"

The mighty Trump Pyramid landed right on the very tip of Ptlnys's big toe. Pan's greatest hero jumped back as if he'd been launched from a slingshot. Up and down he hopped, holding his injured foot and howling in pain. "Aw, the nail's split off!" he complained. "It's already swelling up! It'll never heal right!"

He was lucky it was ever going to heal at all, I thought to myself. Six inches to the left and his whole foot would have been flat as a pancake. Another yard and ***adiós, Mr. Magnificent***.

Stan shot me a look of complete understanding. At least now we knew how Ptlnys got his legendary ingrown toenail. A ten-year-old Earthling accidentally dropped a pyramid on it. Another great zippered mystery solved.

"We'll get you to a doctor," Stan promised.

"Never mind about me!" Ptlnys exclaimed. "Watching your nasal processor in action was the biggest thrill of my life! I'm on the verge of the most important invention of all time! I've got to get back to my drawings!" And he limped off in search of a ride to the Sphinx, complaining, "How come you can never find a sedan chair when you need one?"

"Gthrmnys and I have pooled our natural supergenius to analyze our situation," Zgrbnys informed us. "We have weighed every possibility, counter-possibility, and counter-counter-possibility. We have decided that the best course of action is to *get the heck out of here!*"

"Not yet," I said grimly. "First we have to go back to the palace and bust up every single thing from the future that you two gave the Egyptians."

"It's the only way to repair history and avoid a SPITTOON violation," Stan added.

"But we were co-Pharaohs for years," protested Gthrmnys. "We'll be recognized in a nanosecond in the palace."

"Just act intelligent," I told them. "Trust me, no one will know it's you."

Okay, that was pretty mean. But getting through to those Dummy-Pants could be like drilling into an anvil with a Popsicle stick. I mean, we weren't going to knock on the palace gates and say, "Can we please come in and break things?" Obviously, we were going to sneak in.

We had to walk back to Thebes—three hours, barefoot all the way, mostly on hot sand. **When you get mummified, you're not allowed to keep your sandals.** By the time we crouched in the bushes outside the palace, the four of us were limping as badly as Ptlnys. Even my blisters had blisters.

We climbed in through a small window in the guards' dressing room. Jackpot! Nobody was around and there were racks and racks of soldiers' uniforms. There must have been some pretty short guys working at the palace, because even Stan and I found stuff that fit. Disguised as sentries, we darted off in search of tools we could use to smash things. I picked up a long-handled battle-ax from the armory room.

The Smarty-Pants were busy drawing mustaches on each other with a piece of charcoal.

"You look so entirely different that I must use

my nasal processor to confirm it's really you," chortled Zgrbnys.

"I'm not one-hundred percent certain that I *am* me," agreed Gthrmnys. **"And you're a total stranger."**

We stepped out of the armory into the foyer, where a uniformed guide was leading a class of Egyptian schoolchildren on a palace tour. "And on our left you will notice a statue of Alexander the Great made out of balloon animals. And on our right, we see the co-Pharaohs with a little dirt smudged under their noses."

"Weren't they mummified for spying?" asked one of the kids. He looked about kindergarten age.

"At first we were," stammered Zgrbnys, "but we pleaded guilty to the lesser charge of driving a chariot without a license. So our sentence was reduced from mummification to community service."

"And while we were out painting the tomb of Queen Hatshepsut," Gthrmnys added, "we got drafted. So here we are, ordinary guards, and not fugitives from—*ooomph!*"

I whipped off my headdress and stuffed it in his mouth. Stan grabbed Zgrbnys, I grabbed Gthrmnys, and we ran.

"What should we smash first?" panted Stan.

"The microwave oven," I decided. "Where is it?"

"The royal antechamber," supplied Zgrbnys.

I hacked the microwave in two with one stroke of my battle-ax. Then I pounded the low-fat popcorn into cornmeal, and crushed the egg cooker. Boy, that ax was heavy. It makes you respect those ancient warriors who could swing them around like yo-yos. I was already winded, and the room still had a fax machine, an electric toothbrush, and a Lava lamp that all needed smashing.

I turned to Stan. "Don't just stand there! Help!"

My exchange buddy put his finger in his nose and twitched slightly. The fax melted, the tooth-brush evaporated, and the lamp turned to dust.

I grinned at him. "Your way is better, but mine is more fun."

ANYThiNg you can do, my NOSE can do better.

All through the palace we stalked, destroying everything that didn't belong in ancient Egypt. Nobody hassled us. There were hundreds of guards around; we were just four more.

I bashed up the karaoke machine, the stapler, the Slinky, and the paperweight that, when you shook it, showed a snowstorm at the black hole of Cygnus X-1. Stan's nose fried the Etch A Sketch, the toilet brush, the VCR, and the gum-ball machine. While Stan took care of the Cuisi-nart, I found a pin and popped every balloon animal in the Hall of the Gods.

"I think that's everything," said Zgrbnys.

I pointed down one last gilded hallway. "What about in there?"

"Those are Tutansweet's private chambers," whispered Gthrmnys.

And then I saw it. There, right on the new Pharaoh's bed, sat the Nintendo PlayStation.

Chapter 18
THE SUSPENDERS

"We can't go in there!" hissed Zgrbnys. "It's too risky."

"But the PlayStation contains computer technology," protested Stan. "It would be a gross violation of SPITTOON to leave it here."

That's why Stan and I wound up standing over the Pharaoh's own bed, preparing to destroy Tutansweet's most prized possession.

"Okay," I whispered. "One—two—three—"

"Hello, Your Great Imperial Royalness," came Gthrmnys's loud voice from the hall. "We're just two humble guards who happen to look a lot like the old co-Pharaohs."

Wham! My battle-ax came down on the PlayStation, while Stan's nose shot a bolt of lightning that set the pieces on fire.

"What's that noise?" Suddenly, Pharaoh Tutansweet was in the doorway, staring in horror at the flaming wreckage on the bed.

"My PlayStation!!" The wrestler-sized king drew a massive sword and pulled it back like a baseball bat.

His sword came forward in a home-run swing. Desperately, I got my ax in the way.

SNAP! My weapon broke in two and clattered

to the floor. The Pharaoh swung again, ready to slice us in half.

The razor-sharp blade was an inch from my neck when Stan got his finger in his nose. All at once, the sword went as soft as a wet noodle and drooped to the angry king's sandals.

"Guards!!" bellowed Tutansweet in a blind rage.

We bolted. What a footrace! Four of us against hundreds of soldiers. Every time I looked over my shoulder, there seemed to be more Egyptians running after us. By the time we sprinted out the palace gates, it seemed like half the Egyptian army was hot on our heels. A flaming arrow sizzled past my ear, missing by inches.

"Where's the ship?" I howled. But as I rounded the corner, I spotted the main holding pen for impounded vehicles. Behind a low fence grazed horses, oxen, camels, elephants, and— hooray! **Our Button-Fly 501 space cruiser floated among the livestock.**

Without missing a step, Zgrbnys put his finger in his schnoz to lower the staircase and red carpet. It had to be history's very first full-speed galloping nose pick. We hopped the fence and darted in and around the animals, dodging hooves, and hurdling elephant droppings. Up and into the craft we sprinted. A split second after the door spiraled shut, a volley of arrows rained against the metal of the ship where the opening used to be.

Zgrbnys threw himself into the pilot's seat. "Prepare for liftoff—"

"Not yet!" cried Stan. "There's a malfunction in the navigation computer!"

Gthrmnys tugged at a nostril. "Diagnostic check!" he ordered.

The ship's computer sprang to life like a Christmas tree full of blinking, colored lights. A mechanized voice announced, "There is a used Kleenex wedged in the navigation console."

I was embarrassed. "Mine," I admitted. It had to be. Pants *ate* Kleenex; I was the only one who had any other purpose for them. I found the guilty tissue and yanked it out. "Sorry."

"Imagine using delicious Kleenex to blow your nose into," harrumphed Zgrbnys. "Earthlings are barbarians." He hit a switch, and we lurched a thousand feet straight up, quick as a hiccup.

"Okay," I said. "Now we need a new shipment of Nile Delta goldenrod."

"But that's all gone!" protested Gthrmnys. "It's at the bottom of the Nile in a giant water-tight container!"

"We can still get it," argued Stan, "using the Suspenders."

"Suspenders?" I repeated.

"A robotic cargo-handling system," explained Stan. "It was invented by the Smarty-Pants and built by the Designer Jeans. The Suspenders could pluck out the whole barrel."

Zgrbnys focused the ship's scanners on the Nile. "Hmmm. I see fish, seaweed, Cleopatra's barge, and—aha! A giant piece of Tupperware three hundred feet wide."

"Tupperware?" I turned blazing eyes on the Smarty-Pants. "Where did the ancient Egyptians get Tupperware?"

Gthrmnys shrugged. **"Just because they're ancient doesn't mean they don't deserve to keep their leftovers crunchy and fresh."** He pulled a lever. "Activating Suspenders."

Two long elastic straps plummeted from the bottom of the ship, clips open. They disappeared into the waters of the Nile. Then, a moment later, they sprang out again, clamped to a dripping, mud-covered pink Tupperware tub as big as a football stadium. I don't know how we lifted it. I mean, our ship wasn't a fiftieth the size of that container. But Pant technology was like magic sometimes. The Suspenders clamped the thing to our ship with nothing more than a faint *wump*, and we just kept on flying.

> THEY SHOULD CALL IT
> THE SNEEZY-BOWL!

"That was easy," I said, pleased and surprised. I mean, we had our goldenrod, and our Smarty-Pants, and we were heading back to the future. But I couldn't shake the feeling that we'd forgotten something.

Zoom!! A deadly heat-seeking missile shot past our ship, missing us by inches.

A *missile*? In *ancient Egypt*?

Then we flew out from behind a cloud, and I saw it. It was the B-52, filled with angry Egyptians!

"Prepare for light speed!" Zgrbnys exclaimed.

"No-o-o!" howled Stan.

My exchange buddy's eyes were locked on the main view screen. Dead ahead of us was the Sphinx. There, perched on top of the great stone head, was Ptlnys, chiseling away at his schematic drawing on the nose.

"We can't save him!" cried Gthrmnys. "We've got to get out of here!"

"If that diagram gets lost, the nasal processor might never be invented!" Stan argued. "Then the future of the whole *galaxy* would be changed!"

Suddenly, the heavy stone nose lurched. Ptlnys lost his footing and fell over forward. We watched, horrified, as the nose, and on top of it, Ptlnys, broke away from the statue and plummeted off the face of the Sphinx.

Is that what they MEAN by NOSE drops?

Chapter 19

ESCAPING BY A NOSE

"*Ptlnys!!*"

Heroically, Stan leaped for the controls, knocking Zgrbnys to the floor. The ship shot forward, and the ceiling above us began to open. I saw a split second of the Egyptian sky, and then—

"Heads up!" I hurled myself out of the way just as the giant nose of the Sphinx crashed into the ship, crushing the chair I'd been sitting in. Ptlnys rolled off the stone and landed right in my lap in a shower of dust and pebbles. So much for the great zippered mystery about what happened to the Sphinx's schnoz. In a million years I never would have guessed it was this.

Ptlnys's eyelids fluttered. "Am I dead?"

I shook my head. "You escaped by a nose."

"Oh, no!" cried Stan. "They fired again!"

"Evasive action!" I cried. But when I checked the screen, I could see it was no use. The missile was coming straight at us.

"We're goners!" cried Zgrbnys.

"Now I'll never get to donate my magnificent brain to the Pantsonian," added Gthrmnys tragically.

I closed my eyes.

KA-BOOOOOOM!!!

The explosion was even louder than I expected. But somehow we didn't blow apart into a million pieces. What was going on here? We were supposed to be dead!

I opened my eyes. A dense yellow fog had replaced the bright blue sky. All of Egypt was covered by a thick cloud—*of Nile Delta goldenrod*!

Of course! The missile hadn't hit the ship! It had slammed into the colossal Tupperware container!

Stan closed the roof, but not before a spray of airborne goldenrod covered us. We dissolved into *achoos*.

The Strato-fortress engines sucked in goldenrod.

Pow! Pow! Pow! Pow! Pow! Pow! Pow! Pow!

One by one, all eight of the B-52 jets exploded. Parachutes appeared as the crew bailed out. There were major-league fireworks as the Strato-fortress bomber burst into flame, and blew itself to bits.

Zgrbnys looked embarrassed. "Oh, yeah, we might have given them the parachute, too."

"And a few other items that probably won't change the future," added Gthrmnys. "The TV dinner, the pink flamingo lawn ornament, and—*achoo!*—the handy-dandy radish curler."

The Smarty-Pants replaced Stan at the controls, and we flew up and out of Earth's atmosphere. By this time, the air filters had started to clean up the goldenrod pollen, so we could all breathe again.

Ptlnys regarded us with wide-eyed amazement. **"If you four are a sample of what the future is going to be like, I'm glad I live in the past.** I can't handle the excitement!"

DON'T bE Such a wuss!

"Ptlnys, please don't judge the future by us," my exchange buddy pleaded. "Wonderful things lie ahead, and you are destined to be the greatest hero Pan will ever know. I, Stan, assure you that today was not a typical day."

For once, the Smarty-Pants agreed. "A typical day has much more thinking in it," Zgrbnys explained, "and far less running, yelling, escaping, and narrowly missing getting killed."

"Statistically speaking," added Gthrmnys, "after all we've been through, we won't be due for another big scare for several decades."

No sooner were the words out of his mouth than a spaceship careened into orbit right in front of us, hurtling at light speed on a collision course.

"Look out!" I bellowed.

Zgrbnys dove at the controls and we swerved out of the way. The other ship missed us by a hair.

"More aliens going to ancient Egypt?" I mused. It's amazing they had any room for the Egyptians.

Then I saw the other craft in the view screen. It was flat and eight-sided—another giant stop sign. More visitors from Pan.

"A Button-Fly 1 space cruiser," said Gthrmnys, impressed. "The first of the Button-Fly series. That's quality workmanship. They don't make them like that anymore."

"It's the ship I was waiting for when I found you!" Ptlnys exclaimed excitedly. "My ride back to Pan!"

We docked with the Button-Fly 1, and Stan

and the Smarty-Pants used their nasal processors to move the Sphinx's nose to the other cargo hold. Weird, huh? Nose computers transporting a diagram for the nose computer—which hadn't even been invented yet. If you think about it long enough, it makes your brain hurt. Kind of like calling up Alexander Graham Bell long distance and telling him how to build the first telephone.

What if you got a busy signal?

Since I didn't have a nose computer to do the heavy lifting, I helped the other crew perform first aid on Ptlnys's foot. Let me tell you, I wouldn't have traded places with that poor guy for a billion dollars. His toe had swollen up to the size and color of a plum tomato.

"Well, Ptlnys," said Stan when it was time to leave. "I, Stan, will never forget our time together. May the Crease be with you."

"And with you, Agent Mflxnys," smiled the great hero. "It's refreshing to know that the children of the future are as intelligent and resourceful as you and your Earthling friend." His brow darkened. "I wish I could say the same for your colleagues, the co-Pharaohs."

"We're terribly sorry we fired you from your pyramid-building job," Zgrbnys apologized. "If we had known that you were Ptlnys the Unbelievably Magnificent, and not just another smelly Earthling, we never would have done it."

"All that my partner says is true," added

Gthrmnys, "except he forgot to mention that the whole thing was his idea."

"*My* idea?" cried Zgrbnys. "I didn't even want to be Pharaoh in the first place. I told you we should have taken those jobs as high priests of the Temple of Osiris. But no, you had to be top banana!"

"Oh, yeah?"

"Yeah!"

"Remarkable," commented Ptlnys. **"Centuries pass, worlds transform. But stupidity is eternal."**

He may not have been Unbelievably Magnificent yet, but the guy had a way with words. I stole his line—word for word—for my rules of coolness.

Chapter 20
THE *REAL* FUTURE

As we spun around the Sun, reversing the time warp, I started to get really nervous. In a few minutes, we would be back in the year 2000. What if the future wasn't fixed right? What if it was still Egypt, or something even more awful? We could be savages, living in caves. Fungus could be the only saber-toothed tiger who drinks out of the toilet! Or worse, my family might never have been born at all. I'd be all alone. I might even just disappear the minute we hit Clearview.

"Come on, Earth," I muttered under my breath. **"Be normal."**

Stan was worried, too. "There's more than just Earth at stake here, Devin. If we allow history to change too much, all of SPITTOON could collapse. We'd have people going back in time just to get a bargain on a dozen eggs, or to bet on horses that they know are going to win. Time traveling would be as common as taking a crosstown bus. The future would get changed so often that you couldn't even tell what it was supposed to be in the first place."

"What a couple of worrywarts," sneered Zgrbnys from up at the controls. "Of course the future is secure. You had Smarty-Pants intelligence telling you exactly what to do."

"Don't give me that!" I snapped. "You two were ready to leave without taking care of the B-52! It was pure luck that they attacked us, or you wouldn't even have remembered it was there."

Earth grew larger and larger in the view screen. And suddenly, we were in the clouds, cruising for Clearview. The knot in my stomach got tighter and tighter until I thought I would pass out from the tension. As we came through the cloud cover, I could make out flashes of my hometown. But I couldn't tell if it was back to its old self.

All at once, we were there, hovering low over Clearview. My heart in my throat, I risked a look out the window. Relief washed over me like a wave. There were houses out there instead of pyramids. Cars, not motorized chariots, zipped around on the streets.

"It's okay, right?" I barely breathed.

Stan was too choked up to speak, but he managed to nod.

As we passed over my house, a blond long-eared dog went racing across the lawn. It was Fungus, out playing with Roscoe in the backyard. We were home! Home to the *real* future.

The Smarty-Pants cracked open a roll of toilet paper to celebrate, and even Stan joined them for a square or two.

But all at once, I found myself feeling really sad.

> BREAK OUT THE CHAMPAGNE NAPKINS!

Yeah, I know I should have been overjoyed. It was nothing short of a miracle that we had fixed the future without getting ourselves killed in the process. But I just couldn't get into the party mood. And it had nothing to do with the fact that toilet paper wasn't my idea of a feast.

Stan put a friendly arm around my shoulders. "This is the best we could have hoped for, Devin," he said soothingly.

"But we didn't do what we set out to do," I mourned. "We never brought back any golden-rod to make the tourists sneeze. And we sure can't risk going again. Time travel is like juggling atomic bombs! One slipup and the whole future is wrecked." I had to struggle to keep from breaking ☞ **Rule 18: Whining is for wimps.** "And now I'm going to lose my best friend for the next sixty years."

Stan's fried-egg eyes looked pained. "I, Stan, will get here sooner," he promised. "With good behavior, perhaps I can be back to Earth in as little as forty-five years."

A MEГE SLAP ON THE WГisт.

"Don't worry, young Earthling," put in Zgrbnys. "We will visit often. Each century we Smarty-Pants sponsor a being less gifted than ourselves."

"Just the way we did in the 1900s with that Swiss patent clerk," added Gthrmnys. "The one who played the violin. What was his name?"

"Albert Einstein," Zgrbnys supplied. **"Not a very smart fellow.** But his hair-cut was so stylish."

Stan practically glowed. "See how lucky you are?"

"I'm a regular leprechaun," I mumbled. If there was one thing worse than losing Stan, it was looking forward to a lifetime of visits from the Dummy-Pants. I pictured myself at age thirty-five, explaining those two idiots with their fingers up their noses to my wife and kids.

Didn't it figure? The Smarty-Pants refused to take my advice to land the ship in the woods. They insisted on setting us down in the *same* parking space as before—right in the middle of a line of cars.

"But you got a ticket last time," I protested.

"Which we didn't have to pay," Zgrbnys said smugly. "Why is your primitive Q-class brain so fixated on this?"

"Well, at least put a quarter in the meter," I persisted.

"We only have Egyptian money," Gthrmnys reminded me cheerfully. "I'll tell you what. We'll flip this coin. Tails, we pay; heads, we don't."

I stared at the silver piece in his hand. His own portrait was stamped onto the face of it, beside the hieroglyph for pharaoh. But when he turned it over, Zgrbnys's picture grinned at me from the other side.

"Hey, wait a minute," I said angrily. "They're both heads."

Zgrbnys shrugged. "Well then, I guess we don't pay. Let this be a lesson to you, Earthling, for the next time you think you can match wits with Smarty-Pants."

The door spiraled open and we started down the staircase.

"Achoo!" sneezed Stan.

"Achoo! Achoo!" That came from Zgrbnys and Gthrmnys.

I frowned. What was going on here? And then—

"Achoo!" I sneezed, too.

I looked around. There were yellow spiked flowers amid the weeds in Clearview Park. Flecks of yellow could be seen in every lawn and garden. I gazed down the street to where the woods began. There was almost as much yellow as green in there!

It was—it was—

"Nile Delta goldenrod!" I gasped. "But—but *how*? We lost it all in ancient Egypt!"

I watched Stan's confusion change to understanding and finally delight. "When the B-52 shot down the giant Tupperware, billions of goldenrod seeds were sent flying for hundreds of miles. They must have planted themselves! And

over the centuries, they've spread across the entire—*achoo!*—planet!"

"Do you think the tourists have been sneezing?" I asked excitedly.

Stan put his finger in his nose. I waited with
bated breath.

This was the big moment. Now we were going to find out if Stan would be called back to
Pan in disgrace, or if he could keep his job.

"They've been sneezing like crazy!" my exchange buddy crowed triumphantly. "Customer
satisfaction is higher on Earth than any other
spot in the galaxy—even higher than the beach
at Mizar 2, which has a binary sun, so you can
get a two-sided tan." He reached out to me.
"Give me an elevated five."

"That's 'high five,'" I corrected, slapping his
hand. "Congratulations, Stan!"

"I, Stan, have been promoted to the second
drawer from the top, and my contract has been
sprinkled with red-hot chili peppers so it can
never be eaten," my glowing exchange buddy
went on. "I'll be on Earth as long as there are
tourists—and that'll be a long time!"

We were clamped together in a joyous embrace, pounding each other on the back. I'd long
since changed ☞ **Rule 8:** No hugging to No hugging
unless you've just pulled off a miracle. So we were
safe, coolness-wise.

Then I noticed that the Smarty-Pants both
had their fingers up their noses, frowning.

"What's wrong?" I asked.

"My nasal processor shows that we have an

unpaid parking violation from Clearview, Earth," scowled Zgrbnys.

"I knew you were going to get in trouble for that ticket!" I exclaimed.

"But how could an Earth fine get back to the Grand Pant on Pan, eighty-five thousand light-years away?" said Gthrmnys in perplexity.

I snapped my fingers. "Ptlnys had it! He stuck it in his pocket so the soldiers wouldn't get it when we were arrested for writing on the Sphinx. He must have brought it back to Pan."

"I suppose we'll have to pay it," grumbled Zgrbnys. All at once, he turned pale. "Wait a minute! This fine is over eight million dollars!"

"It was only a thirty-dollar ticket!" wailed Gthrmnys.

I laughed in their faces. "Yeah—when you first got it. But Ptlnys handed it in during the time of ancient Egypt. It's been collecting interest and late fees for three thousand years!"

It didn't take very long for those two Dummy-Pants to hatch a scheme to get the money to pay their debt. "We will travel back in time to the

TaLK abOut a huGE NESt Egg!

age of the dinosaurs," said Zgrbnys decisively, "where we will invest seventy-five cents in Pterodactyls 'R' Us on the Jurassic Stock Exchange."

"Which will be worth millions when we return to the present!" raved Gthrmnys. "Brilliant! I'm glad I thought of it!"

I peered over at Stan and noticed in alarm that he was taking this idea seriously.

"You can't let them do that!" I hissed. "They'll mess up the future twenty times worse than before!"

"Devin," he began patiently, "they're *Smarty-Pants*! They didn't invent thinking, but they perfected it!"

I sighed. Oh, sure, I would probably never be able to convince him that his precious Smarty-Pants were a couple of interstellar airheads. But now that Stan's job on Earth was safe, at least I'd have plenty of time to try.